A SLAVE'S INHERITANCE

Part One: Incognito

Anthony M. Ware

dizzyemupublishing.com

DIZZY EMU PUBLISHING

1714 N McCadden Place, Hollywood, Los Angeles 90028

dizzyemupublishing.com

A Slave's Inheritance
Part One: Incognito
Anthony M. Ware

First published in the United States
in 2023 by Dizzy Emu Publishing

dizzyemupublishing.com

Praise for *A Slave's Inheritance*

"Wow! What a ride. Shocking, sexy and scary, often at the same time. This is erotic horror fiction that pushes boundaries far beyond what most people could dare themselves to imagine."

Andrew Hannon, 13Horror.com

A Slave's Inheritance

Part One: Incognito

Chapter One: Sorry But Not Sorry

The bottom of my feet ached in pain. Every few hours I would slip off into hiding and gently rub them while I wondered how so much pain could be tolerated in this body which my soul had borrowed. The brain inside my skull was screaming for rest.

I had volunteered to be the host and maid for the evening in my own house. Why the hell had I decided to do that? I fought the urges between being and not being a part of the occasion going on that night. With me being only human, my emotions took the lead and I began fighting the thoughts inside my head. My stupid husband and I fell into an argument right before the party and that fight put someone on my bad side.

The moment everyone began showing up at my house, I had taken the initiative to not be a bitch and try to put my best self forward, and not only that, but it was also in my best interest to keep my mouth from saying shit that will cause a hoe to get fucked up. I was not in the best mood. All I could think about was getting into my comfortable king size bed. Looking at my watch, I saw there were two hours left until the occasion was over. Soon as the time came, I'd be kicking all these people I didn't give a fuck about the fuck out. The only excitement that night that almost got out of hand was when the white girl decided to get white girl wasted.

After watching the terrible act she put on, eventually I pulled Tommy to the side and told him to send that bitch home. That had been hours ago. My eyes were fixated on the clock watching the red hand fly away, the big hand moving as if it was a turtle with one leg. Finally, the small hand landing on the exact number I had been waiting for, the event expired. With five minutes to go, I began taking drinks out of the guests' hands, pouring them out into the sink or plainly throwing them away.

When my house became people free, I could feel myself crawling slowly into bed, my head falling in the softness of my cotton stuffed pillow, my waist sinking into the bed. I slowly pushed out a fart and it felt so amazing. I felt better. My body shut down and I gradually flowed into relaxation. I found the darkness behind my eyelids and was soon sound asleep.

The dream that came to me was beyond the real world. It was full of excitement when I saw myself jumping, swinging my arms through the sky.

Looking down at myself, I saw my legs wrapped in booty shorts - the kind that were too expensive to buy but which every hoe still ended up with a pair of. A tightly tied netted shirt fell right above my belly button. My hair grazed through the wind as my arms swung around a silver striping pole. I was screaming "Give me the fucking money!"

A second dream migrated into the dream I was already dreaming. I can see myself standing, watching through a double-sided mirror, looking at myself trying to find my way through grass that was too tall for me to see over. Looking at myself, I was a lost girl trying to escape from terrible men. In their hands they were holding their fat, long, juicy, round dicks. I could hear the throbbing knocking noise from their man tools. I was a slave to sex, meaning I know I was screaming and hollering "You can fuck me if you can catch me!" to make chasing me that more exciting.

Running at me at lightning speed, a sweaty muscular Centaur jumped over me, with his back facing me, his feet standing firm into the earth, the Centaur swinging his sword, lifting his shield. He was protecting me. My jaw dropped to the ground. Everything about the half man, half beast made my nipples hard - veins popping from his arms and chest from fighting, using his heavy shield and sword. The centaur's nuts swung left to right as he defeated the bad men that wanted me for themselves. Those men carried themselves like the type of guys that would make you their sex slave just so their dicks could throb and nut inside some wet pussy.

The big, strong, muscular Centaur marched up to me after his victory, looking into my eyes. His hairy chest filled with sweat and blood. In a strong trumpet-like roar he asked me "You want to taste the dick I was blessed with from the Gods?" My stomach filled with butterflies. "Inside this dick is years of cum build up."

My mouth gained moisture, the muscles inside it working together to find the words to say yes, the earth began to shake and crack. Everything which had been in arms' reach became distant, and those things one by one started to fall into the earth.

Taking a peek over my shoulder to see what was causing all the commotion, I saw Tommy Grey, flopping all over the bed, trolling over me. That damn liquor. This man just wakes me up out of a dream of a lifetime. I'd been seconds away from having my pussy destroyed by a half horse with a human upper body. If I could have counted how many days I had not had sex, I would still be counting numbers walking down to my grave.

Tommy never noticed when I turned my backside towards him trying to ignore what just happened. One of my selectives in school, outside of my academics, was acting, I failed. The simple fact is, I was never good at acting. Today I acted as if I was sleeping.

I said to myself "What the fuck?" I kept my patience while I lay there and ignored his stupidity. Forcing myself back to sleep, hopefully to find the half man, half beast, I felt something poke me on my ass. It did not hurt, it felt soft. Reaching my arms around, it was his dick all over my fat ass. I fell into my bed horny, for him to wake me up for some pussy, the pleasure was all mine. With liquor in his system, I knew we were about to be going rounds, while I screamed in pleasure, and my life. I knew I was about to be screaming. My pussy throbs when I get the idea a man wants to dump his cum inside me, just because he wants to.

I snapped back into reality and was

wondering "Why haven't I started moaning yet, why am I not gripping the sheets, how come I am not screaming, daddy your dick is too big?" The liquor had more control of him than my pussy. Checking, looking over my shoulder I could see his dick was limp. That is why I was not screaming "Fuck me harder!"

Rolling out of the bed and landing on my two feet, I screamed "Tommy!" I placed my knees on the bed and threw my ass between his thighs. After the dream I had, my pussy was prepared to take dick. Someone was giving me dick, even if I had to take it myself. I turned around looking Tommy right into his face. I yelled in a voice so loud I damn nearly lost my soul. I screamed "Hello! Wake up!" His face had no reaction, no expression.

The liquor gained full control of him, he fell over flopping his ass on the bed. Looking at me with mouth wide open, breath smelling like liquor. I looked at him disgusted and said, "Close your mouth and stop getting drunk. You are a pig, you are fucking horrible at getting drunk. Stop doing it."

Me being in the same room with him was fucking impossible. It disgusted me, and I could not even think about being in the same bed with him right now. All of the thoughts I was having made my pussy dry. Pushing Tommy off the bed, I heard a loud thump. I hope it knocked him sober. He stood up looking as if I did something. I pointed to the living area and told Tommy, "Get yo' bitch ass in there and clean up the mess your guests made. I don't see why you are coming in here bothering me. You're not talking about shit and neither is your dick!"

I was past the definition of pissed the fuck off. With me having the room to myself tonight, maybe I could slide back into my big dick superhero dream. Resting my head down onto the pillow, with my eyes closed I could hear Tommy shuffling with the trash bags. Then even that sound slowly became quiet.

I was on borrowed time. Time was falling

behind me as if a man was scratching his nails on concrete, or a teacher scratching her nails on a chalkboard over and over again until her nails fell away and even then, the scratching continued. I, Kacy Grey, spent years and years blue printing a plan that will last a lifetime. It just was going to take time. I had no problem with time - time is like a jail sentence; it must be served.

The very next morning was not as bad as the day before. I knew that because my imagination was dawning on me, both my eyelids struggling to stay open, I thought I was seeing things, spotting a glass of orange juice being carried to me while I was still lying in bed.

"What do you want, Tommy?" I asked with a sound of dread in my voice.

He said "Look, I made something for you."

Sitting up in the bed, I replied, "I can see that."

He took his time to sit down slowly at the

very edge. In his hand he was holding a food tray. On it was toast with a square of butter on each slice, eggs covered in white shredded cheese, and a glass of orange juice.

I placed my hand on his arm, letting him know I appreciated the gesture, but I was still upset. I looked Tommy directly in his eyes, not with a smile but with an ignorant look.

He said, "Breakfast in bed, babe."

In my head I thought, *Naw, bitch breakfast on a banana boat.*

Staying hush was the best thing for me, especially when last night had been such a disaster.

My mouth was dry like the dirt at the bottom of Jesus' feet. I was happy to have something that could quench my thirst. Around this time in a normal relationship, my mouth would be full of Tommy's dick, and maybe then my mouth would not be so dry. I snatched the orange juice, sipping as much as I could until the air filled my mouth.

To spice things up, I surprised my husband.

I tossed the glass cup against the wall, shattering it into pieces. Tommy jumped to his feet, his eyes aggressively jumping from me to the mess I had made.

Launching the quilted cotton sheets from my skin to the floor, I leapt to the floor and knelt in front of him. Tommy had taken one step forward. The center of my pupils focused on his dick. Looking at him in his beautiful eyes with my chin up I said, "Take your dick and shove it in my throat."

Tommy's ego was entitled to be a man so he did as I said.

I clinched a pair of hairy nuts in the palm of my hand while I rubbed my pussy. Tommy's legs grew weaker as he stood on the tips of his toes, his breathing picking up heavily. He fell to the floor with my pussy in his face, his big, throbbing dick in my possession finally. Slowly sticking this dick in my throat, stroking his dick while my teeth nibbled on the tip of his dick. Juices from my pussy dripped onto his face.

"Open your jaw, dumb dog whore."

I reached into his mouth stretching his tongue from the bottom of his mouth, placing it on my clit. I moaned in pleasure "Keep eating that kitty cat."

Tommy shoved his face in my pussy, eating as much as he desired.

Tommy took hold of my body. My eyes fixated on him, I watched his hand come across my face. In a loud roar, Tommy yelled screaming "Don't look at me, slut!"

Tommy rolled my fat ass in the palm of his hands, smacking my ass cheeks until my flesh could not handle anymore I was in too deep, there was no way I was telling him to stop. I did not want to. The electrifying energy surrounded the room, After all these years I finally felt as if I was in the same room as the man I married. Tommy's fingers scratched across my scalp, snatching me by my long hair.

I tended to wonder from time to time if I

married Tommy for the right reason. I always had a thing for a nice, thick, long curvy dick. That day in the school bathroom, when I forced him to fuck me, my mind was already made up that I was making that dick mine for life. My favorite part about Tommy's dick is when he gets really horny, his veins are huge and when those veins graze across this clit, I squirt every time.

I planted my face inside the bed. As loud as I could I scream and announce in pleasure "I like that shit, daddy!"

We started on the floor and slowly migrated to a position I would never forget. Tommy picking me up from the bed, he carried me into the Jacuzzi tub.

My legs hung over the tub while my thighs rested on the brim. My long legs were spread wide open. Tommy grabbed on the base of his big dick, slapping the lips of my pussy, pussy juice going everywhere. his hips turned and twist thrusting deep inside me. With nothing to hang onto, and Tommy being strong, I gently dug my red fingernails into his back. I moaned and screamed in pleasure. I was so close to spreading my cum all over his dick and then…

The phone rang.

Trying to keep Tommy inside my pussy, I said "If you pull out, you can never fuck me again."

He didn't listen. The phone continued to ring and Tommy rushed to answer it, wobbling into the living room.

I pushed my hand under the water. I was only seconds away from squirting, I had to finish. My pussy shaking, I quickly pushed two of my fingers deep in me.

Juices erupted from my pussy, squirting all over the bathtub as my body jerked like I was having a panic attack. I had my hand holding my right juicy tittie, imagining a sexy, thick, white girl biting my nipples until I begged her to stop. My other hand kept my body from going under the water and drowning.

Tommy jetted inside the bathroom.

If he was a superhero, he would have snatched the hinges from the wall. Tommy fell all over the place trying to put on his clothes. I thought in my head *How did things get to this?* Slowly pulling myself from the Jacuzzi tub, being pissed was beyond my vocabulary. My husband failed me again, the thought of him making me squirt. I realized, however, in a short amount of time that in this house you had to expect the unexpected.

"Tommy, what's going on with you? You are running around the house like your dick got cut off and a bitch refused to help you."

I made it known to Tommy he was going coocoo. My pupils bounced back and forth while he moved erratically, The looks of it, Tommy Grey was having a panic attack "Tommy, what is going on with you?" he looked at me, dazed. "The caregiver found my father dead, Tommy paused for just a second, well we must cut this short The guy has no one else. I am sure my father's body is still stuck in that same old chair, that man did not like much but He loved that chair," The more Tommy talked the more he became disappointed

"Kacy, you and my father relationship is not in good standards, you do not like him."

I replied to Tommy "Your ass is his son and you do not even know him. Your ass was not even there as his son, so stop being a bitch."

"Thank you for being a bitch." Tommy replied to me.

That word does something to my ears, that bitch word is like honey to bee. Looking at him in his face, I waited until he stopped crying like a hoe. Honestly, I do have to say I do remember him telling me about his father, but he also told me on multiple occasions how he hated his father.

Checking back on my familiarity of myself I created a scary energy, enough to tell my cock sucking husband I am over it.

Tommy exited the door faster than he came in. I sat there with my head down, holding my chin in my hand. I was disappointed. A bitch could not even get a chance to sit back and think about the dick. Everything he'd been doing, I thought I would be singing the opera. Instead, I was screaming for someone to please shoot me.

Tommy carried the power to do it, just lacked the balls.

Chapter Two: The Funeral

The very next morning I thought I wanted to kill him. Literally drive up to him and stab him in his chest until I fell asleep doing it. Everything around me stirred up in a panic. My husband called me, screaming on the phone. Tommy expected me to be equipped with radar sensors and already know what he was speaking about. Between his voice and the cell phone that kept breaking up, of course it made it difficult for me to make out and understand what he was asking me to do.

His request over the phone had me pacing around the house, my phone in one hand while I was using my other hand, trying to shuffle through some shirts, looking for something that looked half ass decent. Unfortunately, all the clothes that I had were made to make money, and make married guys act funny. I was born slim. I had no care. I was so tempted to walk up into that funeral looking like I was a general manager over every bitch in the streets.

Eventually I found something. I'm talking about the type of sexy that is illegal. I was already frustrated at him while being on the phone.

I said "Tommy, let me have a minute, all of this screaming is not necessary," I was frustrated with him. I was rushing to leave the house, trying to make it to his location on time. My feet shuffled across the wood floor, causing the back of my heels to hurt. *This is why I need a real man, a sexy big dick man, and who is strong, so he can use half of his strength to squeeze the pain from my feet.*

I forgot this house was basically built off sticks and stones. But right then I was focused on getting to this funeral.

On the way out the front door the rear end of my dress got snagged on a piece of chipped wood.

"Shit!"

It turned my dress from 'cute and ready to get my pussy ate' to 'having to toss this bitch in the trash'. I was already irritated and this made it even worse.

I wish there was a man here that could fuck me so hard I pass out, or a sexy female that can rub my pussy until I cannot cum anymore.

So, what did I do? I tossed my phone and began to scream at the top of my lungs. I was so sick of today and it had not made it past twelve o' clock. My morning could not get any worse than this.

Arriving at the funeral with an outfit that made the occasion an occasion, being minutes late made me the center of attention. I did not give a fuck. All these old ass people's eyes were poking out the corner of their sockets. It was embarrassing. But who gave a fuck? Not me.

Tommy called to ask me to be here for him and support him in his time of grief. He was lucky I'd agreed to it. I wouldn't have been so stand off-ish if Tommy would have fucked me like a man should do his wife.

In this fucked up marriage me and Tommy

were breaking all the rules that came with till death do us part. I took my precious time. I had plans and the only way for that plan to work was to be attentive. I had no choice but to deal with his shit for a little while longer. Tommy had to be watched with my own eyes. I'd been planning my blueprint just for him. I spent years planning. Time making sure all the pieces fit, and watching, caculating every move he decides to make.

The funeral was treacherous. The high heels I was wearing were digging into the grass and causing my posture to be uncomfortable. The feeling that crawled on my skin being around all these old ass people, I was uncomfortable standing at a funeral that had nothing to do with me. With everyone crowding the casket, mourning, I stayed back from the crowd. My whole life I wondered why funerals couldn't be rejoiceful, that a loved one is out of pain, sickness, and misery. Half of these people were crying sympathy for a man that was hated, and for some, they hadn't even known the dead man.

The surface around the casket was decorated with beautiful white rose petals. The fucked-up part was that the roses were fake. A person only gets one funeral. Whoever had done that deserved to be in hell. The steel barrel that is designed to give the pallbearers a more appropriate, comfortable way to support the casket had greasy fingerprints all over the steel.

The pallbearers were the ones who needed to be inside the casket for such a poor job. Trying my best to lift up my eyes from these details, I couldn't help but think the music was dreadful too. A better song would not be too much to ask for, would it? I listened to the scratching, broken notes, and years of tar from cigarettes in the singer's lungs. I placed my hands on my forehead. This shit was giving me a brain aneurysm.

My suggestion was not the most positive but that bitch needed to sit down. The first thing that came to mind was getting a jukebox, holding it above my head and turn the volume on full blast. Just to lift the heavy sad spirit out of this circle. Looking around at people that came together to come here, the funeral. I could see the old lady vocals was much appreciated by everyone gathered together. I think the officiate allowed the old lady to embarrass herself, because she needed the extra money.

On top of her social security check, eventually the funeral officiate announced the dinner had arrived for the repast. If I am allowed to speak out loud, in my opinion the only good thing that comes to and from an occasion such as this one, is the food. Now if you are lucky, you can possibly get some good dick to take home. In my situation I do not like waiting, so you can dick me down in the bathroom. My ears were open, and my pussy ready. I'd come to this funeral prepared to get lucky, because right then my pussy needed attending too.

This pussy does not discriminate. I will scissor a sexy widow fast, then release the best squirt all over her pussy. That will be if I get the chance or we can add another body to the party. On occasion, I go and scout myself as a sexy female to perform pleasurable things, such as eating my ass, licking my nipples, I have to admit a female will never satisfy me like a real man can. I'm authentic, not fake. I could not be a full out lesbian. I need something to shake up the pot. After standing among the dead, I was ready to eat and leave.

I watched everyone fill their skeleton cheekbones with food and make side conversations about pointless shit that had no value. I was tired of standing in one place doing nothing so I began walking around, listening to boring shit. I was carrying one plate in one hand and with the other holding my phone, staring off into the next room. I then received an interesting text message.

Looking down at my phone while figuring out how I should reply, I soon realized I was already a mile away from the repast, and just a few feet away from a small white building, that felt like it carried a heavy burden The roof of the building was leaning over, just a few feet away from touching the ground. The property was surrounded by tall forest trees, with old rusted antiques spread across the field. I thought *How interesting.*

When I was just a little girl, my mother always announced to me "You are a very curious little girl. That is good but it can also be very bad." Knowing my curiosity, I had to take a look inside, I had a feeling I was not suppose to go in there. I was always the person who ignored the voices in my head. The building was run down with years of abandonment and - the way I saw it through my eyes - this building didn't need a human to take care of it; it had already taken care of itself. I began to feel uneasy, a feather like feeling jetting down my spine. The weird thing was I felt drawn to be here. My eye picked up movement far in the trees, surrounding the building. My head started to spin awfully fast. My vision began to blur and my body felt as if I was being pushed forward.

A set of eyes glowed in the dark, beyond the trees.

With my feet slightly planted, I slowly turned my head, looking directly at this thing. Whatever this thing was, it felt comfortable enough to reveal itself from hiding. Looking closely, I saw it was a man. His face carried no soul. The body it had borrowed was fading away, His body had no form - no nipples, no dick, no balls swinging between his legs. Even the world around him was pitch black.

"It is beautiful how nature can create man. The universe attends to recreate mankind."

A voice from hell, breathing, pushing the hairs on my neck. Death came from behind me. Whoever it was, he was masculine as fuck. Different noises went off around me - birds chirping, screams, crying... the sounds ringing in my ears, like someone had taken a bell and banged it right next to my ears.

My body folded in half as if I was putting

myself away to be storage, my knees pressing down on the rough grass. I was in so much pain but I ignored the uncomfortable feeling. Taking my two index fingers and pressing inside my earlobes, I was willing to do anything to plug the pain. These harsh devil sounds were killing me softly. With it being so loud, it was nearly impossible.

My entire body was vibrating in a painful, unpleasant way. My ear drums felt like they were about to explode, as if someone was holding them in the palms of their hands and squeezing them like a pair of balls.

Catching a grip of reality and standing to my feet, I looked in the distance but saw nothing.

"It is beautiful, isn't it?"

"What are you doing down here? Are you going to keep ignoring my phone calls? Hey, I'm talking to you!"

Looking over my shoulders, I could see Tommy's lips moving. His voice began to fade in. Tommy sounded worried. My eyes shifted, seeing more than one person. I looked at Tommy clueless, faking as if I was actually paying attention

"What are you doing down here?" Tommy asked.

"Down where?" I replied.

Tommy pointed behind me. I turned around, trying to see where he was showing me. Looking at my surroundings, I was standing inside the old crunchy building.

"Come on! Let's go." Tommy grabbed my hand in frustration, my legs trying to catch up with the speed of our movement.

That feeling to look behind me, I just could not resist. Something told me there was something there. With all my might, I could not resist - I still had to look behind me. The foolish side of me. Turning around looking over my shoulders, there he was - the pitch-black man with no balls, staring right into my soul.

Tommy glanced over at me.

"What do you keep looking at?"

He stopped us for a second then suggested we pause for the moment.

Tommy observed me, looking at me eye to eye.

"Babe, we need to be focused right here, right now. Baby, listen to me. I received a call from a lawyer, okay? Whatever happened back there, leave it. We must be focused, and I am sure by the time me and you arrive home the lawyers will be at our house waiting for us. Something was mentioned about a will that my name was written in."

Chapter Three: Surprise, Surprise

Every single person Tommy met became obsessed with him, especially good-looking men. They all loved to be around him. The men were more into sex, the females wanting a relationship with him.

I can remember the days when we first met. Tommy and I were both in high school. Tommy received all the attention in those days. He was a star on the football team, he was funny, popular, and every girl saw themselves with him. As for me, Kacy, I was quiet and avoided the spotlight. No sports for me - I was more into my books. I wanted to set myself apart from the average hoes.

I wanted to be a regular girl. Every single day I would force myself to stay consistent, determined and focused to get my shit done. Discovering my popularity, it was the person deep down inside of me. My whole goal was to get shit done. That is probably why I really hated school and wanted to get out as soon as possible. I believed

I had millions and millions of dollars waiting on me with my name on it somewhere out there in the world.

The small group of friends I once occupied myself around, they all found a reason to spread rumors about me to each other. Even if the rumor was not true, the one I hated the most was when the bullies of the ghetto said that I was delusional. I hated people who could not dream. Those type of people I just hated. I wanted to cut their bodies up with a fingernail clipper, stuff the pieces in a meat grinder, put the meat in a bowl and play with my pussy with the blood, and save the meat for the grill.

Instead, I kept moving forward. The same girls - years later - I saw them on the other side of the city, living in a shelter volunteering for a free place to sleep. Karma is a bitch.

Truthfully, I had no idea why I had the mentality to be filthy rich. I guess the fact is I was not going to be one of those girls that tossed my body like a seventy five percent off price tag in the clearance aisle in Wal-Mart. For girls or guys. Money is limitless. But money is not even close to being enough. I was going to grow to be a boss, putting fear in people's eyes, a rumble that makes a heart explode. I wanted all the power in the palm of my hands. Months later, not far from walking across the stage with my diploma in my hand, waving it around with a fake smile on my face, that was when I met Tommy, a friend of a friend. Eventually we began hanging out every day after school, a lot of the time on the football field. He was a football star, and soon after I started to play with my pussy at home, in the dark, in my bedroom, imagining he was forcing himself inside my pussy, my clit sliding along the top of his dick, the sensation forcing my pussy to spit all over his man nipples. I tried holding my breath because I knew his friends were listening. Tommy was scared I would be too loud and cause a sex party. Holding my composure as much as possible, my jaws unlocking, my lips getting softer, my mouth opening and gasping for air, his dick digging in the inside of my stomach, taking my breath away.

I watched the juices run down his chest but of course that was just my imagination. Masturbating at school was the most exciting, and the most rewarding. I instantly start making sex faces while my fingers - fighting the inside of my thick thighs - cream from my soft, juicy, fluffy pussy, making it easier for three fingers to get inside of me. My ears listening to the voices while I climax, I needed to get my nut in before my class was over, or somebody's daughter was going to be eating my pussy while another person's son was biting my nipples.

Tommy never really had the style or swag to make my pussy wet, or even just directly turn me on. It was how Tommy was interacting with the guys when they were all together hanging out, with their shirts off, my eyes watching the sweat force their skin to shine like gold. My pussy imagining all those mixed colors of men - dark skinned men, the white skinned men, putting their hard throbbing dicks inside both tight little holes. My favorite style of dick is when it is curved. It touches my soul differently and touches the inside of my pussy differently too.

Have you ever looked at a man and told yourself *Damn I know he would fuck my pussy up, we can fuck on the floor, the couch however he wants it, as long as he works it*? All a man had to do was ask me one time to fuck and the sad part is men fall short of possibilities, so that don't ask men rather stick their dick between their legs. But if one did ask to fuck the meow out of me, I would respond *Hell yes*. Truthfully, I don't entertain men that only have the energy to nut once. No, honey - we have rounds to go.

Well, I felt like that with Tommy his body was not built to handle sex and that is why I cheated on him and men like him. The only possible real reason I waited for him was because I thought I could not see myself with anyone else. Soon that mentality changed.

I was his biggest fan. I attended all football games and practices, feeling emotionally in love. One year on summer break almost all the students in school were rushing to get out of class. It was time for everyone to take a break from learning. Even the teachers were trying to make an exit as quickly as possible. They needed a break from teaching and at our school nothing was easy. Some of us students held the biggest parties - all the cool guys selling drugs, the girls giving our virginity up to our boyfriends, and gay guys getting laid.

The last time we were going to see the school for a while was that night, the last game of the year. Every student supported the school football team. Our town was small so of course the whole entire school showed up to the last game. Small food fights going on here and there, there was even a fight under the bleachers - two girls disagreed on an agreement that was already agreed upon. I know - stupid. To me everybody was having a good time while acting an ass, just for the fuck of it.

In the last quarter, two rival teams going back and forth talking shit, screaming mother jokes, Tommy and another player on the opposite team fells into a shuffle match. Tommy and the other guy threw punches and grabbed each other's helmets, throwing each other to the ground. That fight kind of had my pussy throbbing. A yellow flag was tossed on the field.

One of my friends came to tell me what happened. Tommy said something another player did not like and the football player's boyfriend felt disrespected and jumped on Tommy. The guy was protecting his teammate, who also happened to be his boyfriend. Tommy was the star on the team but for some odd reason the coach was not tolerating his behavior.

Coach was a mean old white man and did not care how good a player you were. Coach kicked Tommy off the team for the rest of the game and put him on the bench. Tommy was upset, storming off the field. The man was built muscular, black, and extremely in shape. I'm sure he scared a couple of people the way he exited the field. He was scary but dang was a girl's thong wet.

One thing about a man - when he gets his adrenaline racing through his body off of anger, he will do almost anything to take the frustration out. Sex is one of these things. I knew this was my time to get Tommy's dick inside of me, maybe forcing his kids inside of me, forcing him to always be right by my side. For a small amount of time even though I felt eager over my plan, I waited.

My legs were shaking nervously. I had to make a move on him as quickly as possible. I had a gut feeling I was going to miss my shot. I left my seat a little too early. Rushing down the bleachers and slowly sneaking into the boy's locker room, paying attention to my surroundings and making sure no other bitch was trying to get the dick I wanted, the closer I got the more my nerves began to jangle.

Wait, what? I stopped. Moving my head a little closer, something did not add up. Inside the guys' locker room, I heard voices. Everyone was supposed to be on the field. I knew what happened - a bitch beat me to the dick I was going to be all over. I had to see who she was and she better be pretty. If she was then I'd join and in but if she wasn't cute then I would kill them both. Most likely the bitch is a cheerleader. Being as sneaky as possible, I stretched my head around the corner, holding my hair back.

Tiptoeing past a few lockers and trying to keep my distance and my face hidden, the more the gap closed the more I could hear things. What turned my head was when I heard the voice of a guy who was not Tommy.

"Man, bro, coach is a bitch for sitting you on the bench for the entire game."

Tommy replied, sounding really upset.

"Coach knows. Without me the game is

going to be a disaster."

"Bro, listen, you cannot be upset. Coach knows you are the best player on the team, and you know that too."

Looking around the corner I watched Tommy's friend pat him on the back. Tommy looked over at him, smiling. Tommy's friend shoved him to cheer him up, that's what the guys did

"I just want to play, bro," Tommy said to his friend.

Hearing Tommy and his friend talk on and on kind of concerned me that they were two boring guys. Then I saw something that was worth watching - the two friends stepping into the shower at opposite ends.

I am guessing the only reason they chose to take a shower that far apart was just in case someone walked in the guys' locker room; these two could not have anyone thinking they were gay. That move made it a little hard for me to hear two hot guys talk and see two hot football players' ass cheeks. For a second my brain had a quick melt down.

Why am I doing this? Oh, yeah! To get some dick! I thought to myself. I moved from my hide out on the other side of the boys' locker room.

What happened next was a deal breaker for me. A sad moment. The real, I thought, is unreal, is real. I had never seen anything like it in my life. My world crashed around me, my jaw fell through the floor, darkness covered my vision, the vessels in my heart stop carrying the blood, my legs broke in half as if I was dry clay and someone took a bat and destroyed me, my bones fell into crumbs of ash, my pussy dried up, all my hopes were gone. I just wanted my head to roll down the aisles and fall in a ditch.

Chapter Four: A Dick is a Sword

I couldn't help but watch. It was like watching a free gay movie that was produced using cell phones. The more I watched, the more I saw every few minutes that Tommy's friend kept making his way closer and closer to Tommy. I paid attention to the man play, the whole scene, perfectly keeping Tommy in a conversation so that he could make his move. That was the very moment for me when time stopped ticking. Tommy's friend moved in on him, clutching onto Tommy's shoulder and pressing his back against the wall. He practically jumped inside Tommy's mouth with his tongue.

Tommy pushed his friend as hard as he could, which was very surprising. I thought he would act helpless, which would have been something to get my pussy excited. Tommy was a pretty boy and the very first time he began coming to this school I heard other students were questioning his sexuality. But I guess after a few kids received black eyes, people stopped questioning him. Nobody wanted to be walking around school with a black eye.

The friend looked Tommy right in his eyes. I bet he was wondering what was going to happen next. Tommy looked at his friend, face to face. He began to breathe hard. What had just happened had his heart racing.

"Bro, what are you doing? I'm not gay!"

"Bro, it's just a kiss!" the friend of Tommy replied

"And I'm just not gay! Bro!" Tommy continued to get his point across.

I admit I had to check Tommy out. He was a hottie, honestly. I had my eye on the friend too. They both had big dicks, and asses I could grip onto when the dick is really good. I could not put together the type of energy that was coming into the boys' locker room. Both Tommy's and his friend's dicks were getting excited after a few seconds. I watch two dicks stand like shoulders. My nipples suddenly needed attention. Their veins bursting from their dicks, throbbing, waiting to be touched.

The friend approached slowly, extending his arm and reaching for Tommy's heavy, juicy, hairy ballsack. He allowed his friend to roll them in his hand and for his friend to gently squeeze them. Tommy slowly raised on his tiptoes.

The friend looked him in the eyes and said "Just this one time. You have some stress to relieve. Who will find out?"

Instantly I figured there was going to be a fight and the whole school would find out about two guys having sex in the guys' locker room. I was excited - this was going to be good.

The only thing Tommy's friend was going to fight was a handful of beautiful, hairy balls. Tommy took a deep breath, slowly letting off his tip toes and closed his eyes. With the shower running, no one was going to hear them and there was enough noise for me to run around the bathroom to peek from around the corner. I looked back at the score board - the game was still going on. With not much time left on the clock, these two were going to have to hurry. I turned my attention back to the boys' locker room shower.

The friend was sucking on Tommy's hard nipples, doing a circle motion with his tongue with one hand rubbing down Tommy's six pack. With the other hand he was already thrusting the base of Tommy's dick while his friend's lips sucked the head of his dick, spit falling onto the floor of the shower. The water creating moisture. Oh, I knew it felt good. Tommy's friend got on his knees and - looking Tommy right in his eyes – urged him to fuck him.

The boy slowly placed his palms on the floor, following the orders of his daddy, crawling around in the shower like a dog on a leash.

"Come here, stupid bitch," Tommy demanded, pointing to the ground and telling him to sit right in front of him. Tommy slapped him a few times across his lips, his friend shaking his ass in the air, silently asking for a big dick to be driven deep inside his stomach. Tommy stood over him with his legs far apart with a ten-point five-inch dick. Tommy slowly slid his hard dick into his friend's tight booty hole. The friend was getting drilled by the best dick in the world, ass up, head back, and eyes rolling to the back of his head.

My eyes flared red. *That dick should be mine right now!*

They were both having fun and truthfully the movie the two of them were making was actually really good. It had my pussy wet and ready to take some dick.

I watched Tommy slowly thrust his dick deep into his friend's stomach, trying his best to put it in his chest. Tommy stood on his two feet, squatting down, giving dick.

That boy was taking all ten-point five inches. The friend needed to clean out. Painting a dick is very embarrassing and the shit stinks. Letting my eyes fall to the back of my head, one of my hands sliding down my pants my other hand squeezing my titties, this shit was turning me on. I was feeling the movie the boys were putting on for me even though they did not know I was watching.

My moans were in control but I guess not enough. My back against the lockers, squeezing my clit. My eyelids blocked the view of the lights shining from the bulbs. The joints in my legs were getting weak and my knees were knocking. I know my body well and I was close to squirting. A louder moan than I expected slipped through my mouth. My panting grew rapidly. I did not want to cum. It was feeling so good. I relaxed my body and let it flow through.

At that very second I felt the juices dripping from my clit, a girl walked around the corner. My legs open, pussy wet, I started squirting and she walked right into it, spray going all over her cute outfit. I paused with my mouth open after I made sure I'd rubbed all the cum out. The sexy cheerleader took her hand and - wiping my squirt juice from her titties - stuck her hand deep into her throat until she gagged. She looked at me and said "You think you can do that again?"

I slid down, sitting on my booty as the girl stretched her legs over my shoulders. Looking up, I saw her pink pussy. I was horny all over again. The girl squatted down, laying her pussy all over my lips. My tongue went straight inside her in an instant. I started to rub my pussy, sticking my fingers deep inside myself.

"I'm about to squirt again," I moaned, the girl's legs shaking on my face.

"Finish for me," the random girl said, looking me in my eyes. I did exactly what the cheerleader said. I finished painting the floor and lockers with my squirt juice, the rest flowing from my pussy. The cheerleader left the guys' locker room just as fast as she came in. That is the way I like it.

Still sitting in my mess, I was too weak to move my neck to extend around the lockers.

Tommy and his friend were still having sex, Tommy pulling on the boy long hair, two rock hard dicks bumping heads. Tommy forced his friend to his knees.

"Suck my dick, suck my fat dick," Tommy demanded. You could hear the boy choking, tapping on Tommy's legs.

I heard Tommy moan one last time. His friend began to choke while trying to suck dick at the same time. The boy was good - seemed to me the boy had some hidden gills somewhere.

Tommy slowly pulled his dick from his friend's throat, cum flowing from his friend's mouth. I sat there and watched. Why didn't I run out, or fold my hands and cry like a bitch? Because it turned me on.

My feelings were crushed, but my body felt horny as fuck and satisfied. I walked out of that locker room with a lot of things on my mind. One of the things was how could I ask Tommy and his friend to have a threesome? But I wasn't that bold back then. Having someone secret in possession meant power. That secret can get you anything you want from a person. It is a weapon.

Before football practice, I flirted with Tommy, trying to get him all worked up. In a sense I guess he flirted with me as well. I put on my favorite pink leggings with an all-white crop top two sizes too small for me. I asked Tommy to meet me in the bathroom, which was easy as one, two, three. We both stuck with the plan of meeting up. I was extremely excited to finally get the dick I deserved.

"Take it off!" I demanded

"Take what off?" Tommy replied.

"Everything."

I slowly placed my hands on the floor. Crouching under Tommy's nuts, I stretched my tongue as far as it could go. Tommy had smooth, lightly hairy balls. His eyes fell to the back of his head. Whatever he was thinking about, his dick was throbbing harder than a heartbeat. My knees were wet. I ignored that fact.

I had no reason to care. I'd been waiting for this exact moment. My sexy fat lips dripping with spit, Tommy's dick was too big to keep up with. Swallowing with his dick half way down my throat, I could barely take a breath. I was forced to breathe out of my nose. I would die for this dick. I had visions of Tommy walking up to me, yelling, yanking on me, being rough, aggressively ripping my shirt off, my titties jumping out like a busted bag of balloons. Tommy getting hold of my breast, licking the tip of my nipple, lightly biting down. I moan as he touches me, like I've never been touched before.

Tommy picked me up off my feet, sitting me down on the small wall outside the shower that is connected to the boys' shower. My legs dangled freely. my pussy wide open. My body felt like it was on top of the world and my feelings emerged. After I'd seen what Tommy and his friend were packing between their legs, I was starting to wonder, *Do all guys have big dicks?* If so, I want it all the time.

Tommy forcefully yanked me around like I was not shit. Tommy was dominant, and he was good at it.

The strong football player bent me over, my breasts dangling on opposite sides of the wall. I knew what type of sex Tommy was into. Was it sex, or was Tommy beating my ass? Tommy took his belt, stretched it behind his back and started to beat me across my ass, continuously. My eyes widened, my head went up straight - this shit hurt.

"Give me that dick! Shove it in me!"

I demanded Tommy to be aggressive. My body shaking uncontrollably, and Tommy did not stop spanking me.

This man wanting to do all these different positions - my body was to its limit. He stretched me across the locker room floor, my hips off the ground, ass all the way up in the air, and my body would not stop shaking. I turned my head to take a look behind me I had to remember I asked for this. The dick scared me, throbbing like it's a heartbeat, dripping pre-cum all over my fat firm booty cheeks. The veins in his body bulged out from his shoulders and chest, Tommy pumping his dick a few times. He was showing me we had rounds to go. My mouth fell open - I was drooling. I wanted to tap out but I couldn't, it was far too late.

Tommy was patient with me and started really slow.

"Give me that bubble booty," Tommy yelled at me. I thought he was another person. That shit damn near scared me. I wanted to squirt so bad, he had me so close. My pussy was so sore I thought I would never walk again. Tommy slid deep inside my pussy, trying to make his dick's head touch my throat. I moaned and moaned until my voice went out. Tommy finished three times inside me. I felt the cum shoot through my stomach, into my mouth. Tommy's dick was exactly as I dreamed. The way he stroked it and worked it was even better.

I had no choice but to stay in bed for a few more days, holding my hands between my legs. I could not stop thinking about the pleasuring, sexy, painful feeling Tommy's dick gave me. My mind was on it for days. Me and Tommy couldn't resist texting each other. The affection was non-stop. We already had a hundred text messages between each other. Everything was consistent.

The entire school found out we were dating. Nobody - I mean no one - could find out about the incident about the boys or I was fucked.

A lot of his friends cracked jokes about us being in love. Tommy was amused about the jokes and my friends repeated to me so many times they knew me and Tommy eventually was going to be together, sooner or later. In the time being I gained new friends. They were some fake hoes but it made my time at school fly like Christmas. School became very easy… just not as easy whenever I saw his football teammate around him, the boy he'd fucked.

I was becoming jealous. I got the vibe his friend was also becoming jealous with the dirty looks he directed at me, the silent shade. One day during school, the football players did not show up for practice. Instead, Tommy and his friends met up in the parking lot behind the school and most of the football team joined them. I had every right to be with my boyfriend, so I went to cuddle him and to see what was up. I was walking into their conversation just in time. I fell into Tommy arms like a white lady getting dick from a black man for the first time, just listening. One of the guys mentioned one of their team players had quit the team that morning and that was why there was no practice because the coach had to find out what happened and why he'd quit a day before a big game, so the team decided to take a break for the day.

I guess I missed the part where the name was mentioned. It never came up the whole time I was standing in their group discussion. But after taking a swift look around it was the boy who sucked on Tommy's dick. I was happy he was gone. Now I did not have to keep a close eye on him. At least that bitch had no access to my Tommy.

A few years later, after high school, me and Tommy decided to get married. I would soon regret this but it was an amazing wedding, almost exactly as I had dreamt of.

The only thing that was not a part of the wedding was an orgy that I still wished to have. It was mentioned in a conversation, just not really talked about. Besides that, I had other things on my mind.

"Bae, where is that one kid that left your football team? He just stops showing up."

"Uh, I don't know. He did just stop showing up, huh? Well, none of us at the time really cared," Tommy replied.

I did not care if it was a guy or not, I already

knew Tommy was bisexual I had no idea he liked guys far more than females. I caught Tommy texting someone and the messages did not make sense, which made me think there were messages getting deleted. This mysterious person I caught him texting was a female. Well, the name was saved under a female name. When I was reading the messages, the person sent a text saying they missed the football team and how sorry they were for walking out before the big game. Another text from them was talking about the sex in the shower and how it was really good. It was definitely that kid from back in the day.

As I recall, I, Kacy, was eating pussy and two other boys were having sex in the middle of a football game. I knew at that very moment who he was texting. I did not care, I just wanted the truth. At that time I was not being a friend or a wife, and Tommy was not being a husband. I gathered all the information possible from those text messages; Tommy is a professional cheater and liar, now I know why his sex is so bad.

Tommy had my temperature sky high; I was fighting to put my best self forward but he would not stop telling me lies. I wanted to tell him about all the girls I'd slept with. Even then he would still lie about all his affairs. The man just kept going on and on, feeding me more excuses than a bitch on her period. I was so sick of his mouth, I just wanted to reach over and snatch it off.

I excused myself and went upstairs to the bedroom. I plopped down on the bed and just sat there. I had to clear my head before I did something bad, and it was too soon to act right now. A plan is what I had for him. I needed the right time and moment. I could not get caught.

Taking deep breaths in and out, clearing my thought process, I did not want the night ending like this. When I went upstairs, Tommy had to bring his narrow ass upstairs right behind me. Sometimes when I am irritated, I do not want to be asked *Are you okay?*

Duh, bitch! I am not okay. If I don't explain myself, or try to work out the situation, I am not okay and I am just fed up.

If I did not walk out the house, I would be giving Tommy his blueprint present early. I needed to take a long walk. Leaving the house was the best thing I did all day. Not even two miles down the road I was out of breath. Wheezing and chest pumping, a bitch needed to sit down. Sweat flowed down my chest and ass crack, and my ass cheeks were burning.

After catching my breath, I bent over to stretch my lumbar. Naturally I looked through my legs while letting my neck hang. It felt so amazing. Either I was seeing things or being pranked, but there was another pair of legs standing right behind me in the far distance, watching me with my ass in the air. I quickly stood straight up. I turned around and I did not see anything. It was time for me to go back home anyway.

Standing at the door and punching my

passcode into the dial pad, I heard laughing from two different people inside my house. Busting through the door and speed walking around the living room corner, I saw a man standing in my living room. Automatically I thought that these two had just got done fucking while I was only away for thirty minutes. I smacked my lips in disappointment.

I started to walk away. That was when Tommy said "Honey, come here."

I stopped for a second. After Tommy looked at me for the second time, I began making my way to their little conversation. This other man's eyes were weird looking. His pupils were missing. Many voices began to play in my head, over and over again.

"It's beautiful, isn't it?" it echoed. "It's beautiful, isn't it?" It just would not stop. "It's beautiful, isn't it?"

Interrupting the conversation, I put one finger in the air like any given Sunday.

"I'll be right back."

Telling Tommy and our guest in the most appropriate way possible, I stormed off as quickly as I'd came, running up the stairs to my bedroom and shutting the door. There was a knock on the door a few minutes after I had to excuse myself, the same words repeating in my head. Pressing my index fingers in both my ears, the words would not stop. What the fuck was going on? I'd heard the same exact words at the old white building.

Hearing the squeaks as the bedroom door was slowly being pushed open, Tommy's brown shoes were the first thing I saw, even though they were a bit blurry. My entire surroundings were moving in slow motion, my husband bending down and putting one hand on my back as he tried to comfort me.

"Babe, what happened? I thought we were doing this together."

Tommy's words were not as clear as before. I could read lips really well so I watched his lips.

Then I replied "Just tell me what happened."

Tommy grabbed my hand, locking his fingers with mine.

He had given me the love and affection I needed, but he still did not know what was going on with me. It was deeper than what you can see in reality. Tommy seats next to me on the bed. He grazed my chin with his hand, turning my eyes towards him. He told me everything that was discussed between him and the other guy downstairs. Then he said "My dad was not that bad of a guy, I guess," shrugging his shoulders.

Taking a look into Tommy's face, his statement confused me. After all, the stories he had told me about his father were usually about how much he hated his father. Now Tommy was telling me he wasn't that bad of a guy.

I took my head from his hand.

"Go on," I said to him. He was looking as if he had more to say and I was interested in what else he had to tell me.

"There is a church in the next town over. Now, some of the information that was extended to me, that building is part of my family's. It has been passed down for generations."

I was curious about the building Tommy was speaking of. I wanted to go and look at this place. Maybe there was some cash value to this inheritance.

Tommy led the way, but if anything, that triggered me to step in and take over. The drive there was interesting. The closer we drove to the white church, the more things became more familiar. Sitting up in my seat, I began to notice things.

This was the same location as the funeral. Driving down on a two-and-a-half-mile gravel road, my stomach turned and fell into my bladder as we pulled the car to the front entrance of the church.

"Babe, this is the place you ran off to," Tommy said in a joking manner.

I had no idea this was a church. Tommy

acted surprised himself.

I felt like the church had something attached to it, with no front doors, no windows, and definitely no soul. I was standing in front of the building, looking straight through the entire church, almost as if it was gutted. So many holes and cracks made it easy for the wind to whistle.

"What the fuck?" Tommy expressed out loud.

I turned to look at him, like *Yes, you are exactly right, your pops left you a cardboard box.* I was startled but amazed how long this place been standing.

"Babe, how long has this been here?" I asked Tommy.

"One hundred years," Tommy replied, looking at me from the corner of his eyes. Behind Tommy I saw a sign that said 'Condemned'.

"Kacy, I'll be back. Go look around and see if you can find something. I need to go see how much this place would even cost to renovate it before I can sell it."

I waved him away, paying him no never mind. I was in shock. I'd never seen a place so out of shape. Shuffling through the first half of the church, I found nothing but ash and dirt. Standing in the middle of a gutted church did not feel so pleasant. Maybe it was a bad idea to stay behind.

On my way out the door, a thump came from below my feet right at the door way. I leapt backwards. I stood there for a second, looking down at the floor with my eyes squinting, trying to capture another sound but there was no second noise. I was thinking *How is there a basement?*

It was built like a slave house. I made my way to look for the stairs going down. To walk wall to wall inside the church was seconds.

As far as I could tell there was not much to look at. What I did want was some fresh air. Right when I tried to walk out the door, a thump hit below my feet, shaking up my toes.

What the fuck was that?

Either I was going crazy or there was actually a second level, or some type of basement - maybe a storm shelter. I rushed outside to see if my husband was still here but I did not see the car. Tommy had gone. Lurking around the church, watching every step I took, I had no idea what was out here.

Finding my way back to where I had started, in the front of the rotten building I fetching my phone from my pocket. The ringer would not shut up. I figured it had to be my husband. I answered the phone.

"Hello!"

"Hello!" Tommy replied.

"Honey, you're cutting in and out."

Whatever Tommy was telling me, I had a hard time making it out. Not even a second later my phone dinged with a text message.

Tommy texted me *There was a wreck on the freeway, the way traffic is backed up it it's going to take me a few hours to get back.*

I had no reason to respond. With Tommy, always expect something to go wrong. I didn't have a choice to walk anywhere. I was in the middle of nowhere.

Standing in one place with nothing on my mind, I found myself looking at the ground far longer than I expected, but what I also spotted was a small snake that looked as if it was stamped on something. I had to get a closer look. Squatting to my knees, I brushed away the debris. The metal door had snake stamps in a complete circle. Scrambling through the debris, finding the handle, I thought to myself that this was what I had been looking for.

Chapter Five: Demons Have Dicks

It was really dark. I leaned inside as far as I could without falling through. It was far too dark to see anything. Good thing they invented cell phones. I used my flashlight to see and it revealed a spiral staircase. One foot after another, taking it slow, waving my flashlight around, this place seemed to me as if it had been a living quarters at one point, or just a really big storm shelter.

The stair rails were covered in spider webs, a layer of spider webs going all the way down. I could no longer see the light from the sky; it was just this dark place and my flashlight. I knew I was in deep. Why hadn't I thought about checking my battery life before coming down here? I looked at my phone. Shit! It was surviving on ten percent. I had to make this as quick as possible.

I was searching for anything that carried any information about this church or even my husband's family. All this talk about an inheritance didn't make any sense; I'd been married to Tommy for ten years.

With the cracks and the wind blowing, the dungeon was full of sounds, making it hard to concentrate. I never did well in the dark. The first thing I noticed being down here was this awful smell. Checking my phone my battery life, I saw it went down to eight percent.

Fuck, I still haven't seen anything interesting.

If what Tommy was saying was true either slaves lived down here or this was a grave site for the slaves. Or someone built this to keep something or someone away.

With only six percent battery life remaining I finally found something.

The table I saw was super old. The legs were made from broomsticks and the top made out of an old wooden door; this was definitely a slave shack. I started off shuffling through the papers and books, trying to find valuable information. The palms of my hands and fingers became covered in dirt. Wiping the build-up off onto my jeans and checking my battery life, I was down to five percent.

Shit, I got to get out of here.

I heard a small noise. I could barely make it out. It was different than the wind sliding through the crevices. I stopped for a second but now I heard nothing. I had no time to waste. My phone was on the verge of dying, then the noise happened again. This time around it was loud. It was a hissing sound and right behind it was another sound - a loud squeak, as if something was on its death bed, trying to breathe.

I was being dumb but I had to see what the fuck this noise was. I slowly made my way to a place I should not have, farther in the dungeon. I quickly placed my phone onto battery saver mode. Walking slowly, being as careful as possible, my toe hit a hard surface, forcing my phone to fall from my hands.

Fuck! Now I cannot see a fucking thing. This

cannot be happening right now. Why in the hell did I just not leave?

I began to experience a panic attack. I began wrestling around on the concrete floor, feeling around for my cell phone, blinded by darkness. My phone was not what I found. In my hand, between my fingers, someone's feet were in my hands. The skin created moisture, making this thing's feet slimy. With my hands going higher and higher, I was standing on both my feet. Every breath this thing took, the air pressed against my soul. Death was staring me right in the face. This thing, its flesh felt like vertebrates outside its protected skin. Whatever this thing was, it was far from alive and also far from dead. It moved quickly from under the palm of my hands.

The heart that is supposed to be safely rested in my chest stopped beating. The air I breathed became thick, making it hard for my lungs to take in and push out. Whatever was down here with me felt intimidated so it placed me back where it felt it had more power over me. A strong force pushed me to the ground and I screamed, my stomach and chin smacking the concrete floor. This demon began taunting me, blowing on my hair, blowing inside my ear.

"Stop! Stop!" I screamed at the top of my lungs. I was not scared, just blind.

The flashlight on my phone lit up the darkness around me. My phone was sitting in the corner. It had slid farther than I thought. I was too afraid to stand on my two feet. I had no chance of winning in a devil's den. Afraid or not afraid, if this thing had wanted me dead, I would be dead. Pulling my mind together, I had to find a way out and I was not going to accomplish that.

Lying flat on my stomach, I got the strength to push myself up. The hissing sounds were filling the dark room once again. Turning around, there was king cobra, standing high as it allowed itself to stretch. The eyes held no color. Its tongue was missing but it still had the ability to sending a warning to its prey. I began slowly backing up, trying to keep my flashlight from the snake's eyes. My phone had zero battery. The more I inched away, the safer I was.

What is that sparkling object in the corner?

As I lifted my flashlight higher to get a better look, I realized it was a metal box. I wondered why it looked so well-maintained and what was inside it.

The snake held its posture as it watched me examining the metal box. It started to slither around it, turning its small head as if something was speaking to it. The king cobra pushed the box forward slightly, as if it wanted me to have it. It made its final hissing sound before it slithered away.

Fuck. The box needed a key to unlock it. The flashlight to my phone shut off. Damn, I needed to get out of here. Fidgeting with my phone and trying to get it on without success, getting out of this dungeon was my first priority.

I found myself wondering why my husband hadn't come looking for me. I mean, I can answer that question - we are not the kind of couple that do shit like that.

What a shame and what a waste of a man.

If blind people can get from point A to point B then I figured I could too. And I was not going anywhere without this box. Holding onto the box with one arm, with the other arm I felt around as I took each step with caution. A light began to shine through, flickering. I was so relieved I could finally get out of there. My stomach was empty, my pussy sweaty, and a bitch missed her bed.

A voice whispering my name.

"Kacy. Kacy."

Whatever it was wanted me dead but also something down here wanted me alive. Something wanted me to have this box and whatever was inside had a purpose.

My head felt a little uneasy. The darkness around me began to spin at a rapid speed, forcing my brain to rattle and cause me to be extremely busy.

My back fell against the wall. The shiny box became extremely heavy and it rolled from my arms and onto the ground. Footsteps headed towards me at an extreme speed. It was so dark. I could not see anything. I pushed myself from the wall, my head still spinning. The footsteps were getting closer and closer. With no warning, a force tossed me across the dungeon floor.

The pain rushed down my spine, spreading throughout my entire body. I began stretching myself, using both arms to pull myself across the floor. The shiny box laying on its side was now open. I pulled and pulled myself until the box was in my hands. Pressing myself off the floor, I threw my body against the wall; my entire body was in so much pain, there was no way I was able to stand on two feet.

The dungeon began speaking to me. Voices forced their words into my ears, the cries and screams filling up the emptiness in the room. A flash of footprints ran across my view. My eyes could not believe what they were seeing - a little black boy stood face to face with me.

So cute. Innocent. Just a tiny little boy. In a small voice, the little boy said "Help me." The pupils in his eyes went completely white, his tiny little head falling back. The ground around me began to shake, jerking my head back. The little demon boy's body span, acting like a hurricane as the voices of many chanted "It is beautiful, isn't it?"

"What is beautiful!?" I screamed.

The room filled with lights. Eating tables took formation - silver spoons, mantel, candles forming on a white table cloth, humans dropping out of the air, landing in their seats, laughing, screaming. Hacking filled the room between these men. An all-white man was seated at the head of the table, a Cuban cigar between his teeth.

The white man spoke with confidence. Any woman could tell he was a leader, the one with the nuts between his legs, the way he sat at the table, shoulders high.

Two white men stood in the corner with rifles in their hands. One of the guards had an eye patch. The head boss spoke really loudly.

"Them niggers are tasty. Nobody delivers us fresh niggers like Clauneck."

A white man from the other side of the room tossed a hand in the middle of the table. He said "Except this nigga. He tasted tangy."

The man rose from the shadows. Seeing his face made me stand to my two feet. That was Tommy's dad. He was the leader of this organization. He'd just tossed a black man's hand in the middle of the table. Tommy's dad was giving all the orders. So, Tommy's dad was not a slave. He owned them. This is what some of the spirits wanted me to see. They knew I was married to Tommy.

Feeling a little light headed, my stomach grew uneasy. There was puke flowing from my body and I couldn't stop throwing up. I lost all control of myself. My body felt extremely dehydrated and the joints between my bones were weak. After seeing this, I was ready to die. My body collapsed on the floor, falling inside a puddle of blood mixed with puke.

I had no reason to be alive, no foundation for me to stand on. Satan himself was going to go after Tommy. They are going to kill him. Using all the strength I had left to push myself out of my vomit, I crawled through my mess and tried to get a hold of myself. Not looking behind me, I felt my foot hit something hard. It fell to the floor and shattered. It sounded like a vase.

Only a little light remained. It was enough to discern tiny bones scattered across the floor.

Oh my God, these bones are the kids I heard running around.

There were pictures below the kids' bones. Brushing the bones from the pictures, I flashed through the photos.

Sweeping all the picture from the floor and stuffing them inside my pocket, I had survived the dungeon of hell. It was time for me to exit as quickly as possible while I still had the chance.

The air was as soft as cotton. The breeze comforted me like a warm blanket on a freezing day.

I made up my mind to hitch a ride but, looking behind me, I saw Tommy standing in the corner, as if he was a six-year-old boy.

"I have been waiting for you."

Tommy's voice was far from his own. I had spent so many days in that dungeon that I knew the difference.

Slowly walking toward Tommy, I chose my words wisely and spoke really slowly. I knew he was not himself.

"I was in here the whole time. I was screaming for help."

A small little girl's voice replied, coming from inside the church.

"I tried to explain to Tommy, he just did not listen."

"Don't start with me. You've been away from the house for a week and I've been sitting right here waiting for you. And now look what you have done."

Something in the trees was moving around, catching my attention. I turned my head to look. The tress were waving back and forth but I couldn't see anything. Turning around to finish the conversation with my husband, Tommy was already standing in front of me. Looking at him up and down, he seemed to be of himself. He tried to embrace me but I was too far out of my mind to want to feel comfort. The only thing I wanted to feel was that leather seat under my ass and the car taking me home.

Feeling the bumps underneath the tires was reassuring. We were about to get home. I was in need of all type of things – food, because my stomach had not stopped growling; a shower, because my pussy was smelling like the bottom of a lake; sleep, because my body was on the verge of falling into a coma; and some dick, because I was horny.

In my peripheral vision I watched Tommy scrunch his nose.

I could smell myself and it was not easy wearing these panties.

Tommy glanced over at me.

"What is that box you're holding on?" Tommy asked.

"I don't know. It came from your father's church where you left me."

Tommy looked away quickly.

Pulling into the driveway, I saw a tall, olive skinned man with his hands crossed over his shoulders, smiling and waiting at our front door.

Before the car came to a complete stop my feet were already out of the car.

"Sir, what the hell are you doing at my

house? Can I not help you with something?"

The stranger did not move one inch. Not even a change in facial expression. When I got a bit closer, he took one step down from the porch with that smile still on his face.

Tommy tugged me by my shoulders.

"Babe, babe."

I turned around.

"What?"

I did not have time for any weird shit.

"Let me take care of this," Tommy replied.

The stranger calmly raised his hand, silently telling us to be quiet.

"You both will need to take care of this," the stranger said to me and Tommy. Still smiling, the stranger approached me and Tommy. His shoulders were now touching our shoulders. He was so close that he could have kissed us both at the same time.

"We are all a team now," the stranger whispered to us.

He walked slowly away, taking his time

down the driveway.

When we entered the house, Tommy started with his bitch conversation, talking to me like I had shit on my face.

"There is nothing there. What are you looking at?" I asked Tommy. I was on the verge of snatching the olive off his face. I know he felt what I was feeling from that strange guy. I had no time for this I disappeared up the stairs. I had to get myself together.

Tommy yelled "I will make you breakfast!"

I had no idea why he felt like he had to cook for me, but a bitch was starving.

My brain accumulated thoughts. Trying to make things that made no sense connect with reality right now was like me trying to grow wings and fly. Everything had started since the death of Tommy's father. Sitting on the edge of the tub naked with the steaming hot water blazing from its tube, I could hear the stairs creaking. Tommy could not resist. That man had to interrupt my thinking.

Tommy could deny it but he hated to be alone. He tried to open the bathroom door but I had been smart enough to lock it. His frustration got the better of him. As he pulled at the knob and the door shook, I screamed "What, Tommy?"

He started to knock. I thought he was trying to get on my nerves.

Tommy replied, "Babe, I miss you, let me come in."

By the time I'd washed my pussy and gotten out of the shower, Tommy was sitting on the counter top waiting for me and holding breakfast in his hand. I continued down the stairs, right to the food, not to him. I stuffed my mouth with bacon, croissants, strawberries and a glass of apple juice.

"Kacy, calm down," Tommy said.

I had nothing to say back.

Chapter Six: Sex Addiction

What is a sex alarm? It is when a man has a rock-hard dick that will throb when he needs to release his cum build up. When a man experiences that, it is mostly natural or because the man is in a wet dream. And the only way to release the pressure is for that man to have sex at that given time. With a girl or a man, just in case some people are wondering. If you decide not to have sex with that man because you are upset, he will cheat on you.

Hopefully that man can get you to squirt before you can fully come out your dream. If not then it is okay just act like you nutted. Make sure you make all the noises, but not too much because then they'll know.

Tommy was thrusting deep inside of my pussy, just how I like it. As much as the time was getting closer and closer for me to kill him, that dick that morning purchased him some borrowed time, but getting rid of him was far out of the question.

We both had our routines. Every morning he did him and I did me. Once he nutted deep in my heart, he was ready to bounce. Well, after he'd laid on me for a few minutes. He was whispering all in my ear, talking about "Baby, I love you" and turning my head against his bullshit. He did not appreciate my reaction. While he got ready, I went to the bathroom to flush the cum from my pussy.

I heard yelling from downstairs.

"Babe, I am heading off to the gym. See you later!"

I did not give two fucks about Tommy telling me what he was doing. He was really interrupting me taking a shit. I'd purchased a new soap for females that had just come out. I was excited to use it. I had a sexy female coming over and she wanted to eat my ass and pinch my nipples at the same time.

This hookup told me she wanted to show me something new. When she told me what she wanted to do I could not resist. As I mentioned, me and my husband had our own lives. Our bodies lived in the same house. I'd record what happened for him to watch later. That was our only rule - you must record what went on.

Going to the gym was a hobby for me. For me, Tommy, staying in the best shape in my life wasn't a question. If I could I would take the opportunity to live inside a weight room. I know that about me because I have done it before. In my darkest hours, people around me always paid attention to me the day I decided to get back into my best self physically. I envy the way sexy men and girls look at me. Mostly they look at my dick. I purposely don't cum when having sex with my wife.

The hypnotizing begins when a guy or a girl finds me attractive more than they do their own boyfriend or girlfriend. The moment you show me disloyalty in your current relationship then I will know we are on the same page - easier for us to cheat. My routine when arriving to the gym is joining the yoga group. It is always the perfect opportunity for scouting my next sex partner.

I will never have sex outside the gym. People who lack the ability to work on themselves lack the ability to have a nice body and even good booty or pussy. That's where me and my wife see differently. I give her my dick on my time but she falls short of my requirements. In high school she did the things I like. Now she has no consistency. The majority of people ignore looks or ignore the feel of the body. Not me when I sleep next to you. I want to feel hard work to the body, a tight booty hole, and a nice tight pussy.

Ninety five percent of the time I punish my lungs with a hard long run on the treadmill. Two hours, always. My lungs are fighting to keep pushing, my legs striving one step after another, pushing at a rapid speed. The vessel of my body growing heavy, my panting hanging on by a thread.

The pain became addictive, like an addict fighting for his last hit off the pipe.

My pores filling with sweat, the olive skin of my body shining bright as sweat rushes down me, falling into the creases of my tight structured body. The muscles around my calves grow tighter and tighter, making it almost impossible to bend my legs. My body is crying to stop but my mind refuses to listen to the pain.

One minute and thirty seconds left on the treadmill I looked over and my cell phone was lighting up. I watch it as I finish up the last few seconds. I watch my cell phone stop ringing. There's ten seconds left on the clock trying and I'm trying my hardest not to be focused on my phone.

The time was up. I had completed my two-hour run and that was just the beginning of my workout.

I just had a feeling it was Kacy and I was not ready to be bothered by her, at least not yet. I always prepared my mind before putting myself in

Kacy's presence. My mouth was dry like the antelope valley. Bending over, reaching for my sports water bottle, I noticed an extra muscle in my biceps. Stepping closer to the mirror I noticed things about my body I had never noticed before. I noticed my body was sexy as fuck.

I was definitely in love with myself. Looking in the mirror I said to myself I am perfect, even if my wife hated me. She had her reasons. A lot of the reasons of her hate towards me I don't totally agree with but then I grew to have my reasons why I don't give a fuck.

I had to have been really focused scrolling through my phone. I had messages and missed calls longer than Santa's wish list. My eyes were glued to my phone, reading text messages and replying back to them. My neck began to hurt having it down for so long. I just needed a quick look up to relieve some of the pain. Standing behind me was the light that made my day bright.

Looking at her reflection in the mirror, my

eyes running down her body pass her thighs, seeing every curve she was blessed with. She was sexy as fuck, the type of sexy that makes me weak in the knees. The girl was stunning. Perfectly built, slim in the right places. I knew she was dating or married to a black man. To get an ass like that she was taking black dick. Looking at her I could tell she was the type to yell at you and tell you to fuck her in the middle of the day. That was exactly what I had in mind.

"Gym day for that fat ass, huh?" I said to her. She eyed fucked me and that was enough for my dick to get fully hard.

"Yes and no," she replied. I was relieved when she found my comment pleasant. I learned to test the water with words, like make a comment, wait and listen to the response, then watch their expression. I had taken a seat on the bench press. During my workout she stood over my head, her fat juicy pussy sitting in my face.

Filling my ears with information about

herself with her nonstop talking, I could sniff out she had nobody to open up to. I found this weird because she was so sexy and in shape - any guy or girl would want to fuck her. Pain is beauty and she was going through a lot of it. She shared with me, telling me how her husband upsets her on purpose just so he can have a reason to run off and cheat.

So, she felt as if she needed to do the same thing her husband was doing and was sure that if she did then she would not feel so alone. In my head I told myself "You picked the right dick to jump on."

I listen to her stories and complaints. I told her "Working out helps with the stress. That's why I come to the gym so often. You should try it."

"I come to the gym but I never see you."

The woman went for a few squats. In front of the mirror, taking every dip slow and looking right at me, my dick could not take it anymore. Slowly I came up behind her, sliding my fingers slowly up her thick juicy thighs. We watch each other through the mirror, turning each other on. My hand slides up her waist, touching her stomach, my fingers squeezing her nice, round, hard nipples.

Her bottom lip tucked under her teeth, her hand reaches behind her, taking a hold of my big, juicy, hard, throbbing dick. My dick was pushing through my all-black gym shorts. My waist begins to move. I was grinding on her fat juicy booty, my dick bending, going up and down. Softly, she moans. Kissing was not my thing but with her I put my fat lips onto her neck and tried to suck the blood out.

Jerking and twisting her body around to face me, I slowly begin stripping her, pulling her thong below her knees. Her fat ass moved in so many ways. It was so soft and my patience grew thin. I was extremely horny. The bitch wanted to fuck me as well as I wanted to fuck her. I bent her over the weight bench, her fingers touching her toes. She reaches around and began rubbing my hard throbbing dick against her pussy lips. I slowly pushed inside her soft, tight, wet, creamy pussy.

"Fuck me harder," she moaned and screamed and I did exactly what she asked me to do. I beat them guts up.

Placing her on her backside and keeping my dick still inside her, I squeezed her firm breasts. She begs me not to pull out. She is moaning "Cum in me. I feel it coming, cum, daddy!" The way it felt inside her it was almost impossible to pull out, and I could not take the risk. But the pussy was good enough to not pull out, my dick jumping inside her, releasing my cum in her guts, my dick pulsing.

I could not pull out. She was way too good and tight. The way she was screaming I am guessing her husband is not very big and this was definitely a desperate move, especially is she had never taken a big dick; my presumption was obviously wrong - she does not have a black husband. Pulling my dick from inside her, cum came flowing with it. I was done and ready to go to the house.

In this time of my life, I did not have shit, not really a lot going on for me. I figure that is why I spend so much time in the gym. My body is something I gave myself and nothing can take the feeling away, the way I feel when I see my reflection in the mirror. Before I walked out the exit, she gave me her number. The second she turned away I got rid of it. I handed over a little of my time to her, even though I was the only one benefitting from it. I told her I was married and happy. I told her a fucking lie. I just wanted her to know my marriage was better than hers. I wanted to make sure she feels tiny deep down.

I could see my car the moment I stepped outside the gym. The sun was beaming with heat and blinding with its brightness. A very sexy man approached me. His shoulders were sitting high and his head was stiff - he was upset about something. The man screamed at me.

"I know my wife is in there and I know she fucked you or you fucked her!"

Looking the man right in his eyes, I read his unstable thoughts.

"Why would you say that to someone you don't even know?" I asked.

I had taken a few steps backwards - not because I was scared but because the man was spitting as he was talking.

He replied "Because I am the one who sent her ass in there."

"All I did was look!" But in my head, I was like *Thank you for that because that was some good pussy.*

Either my brain is in shock or he heard what I just thought.

His eyes went down to my lips. This guy was like me or found my aggression a turn on. We were so close I could feel his energy through his lips. I felt his soft breath slightly remove from his mouth. He said "I might have set you up."

Smacking my lips, I just cannot believe what he is telling me.

His eyes gave me the energy that he liked rough, aggressive sex. I had to look away for a second. The second I did, I spotted the woman walking out the gym, looking like she was coming our direction. We both kept looking at her. I have to say, she was a beautiful woman. Just as beautiful, while the sun beat down on her titties, my dick was getting hard all over again.

Me and this sexy man both took a seat inside my car. Not a minute after, he began reaching for my hard dick. I moved as far as I could, which wasn't very far. I had a choice to get out but that was the thing - I wanted him to touch me, I just wanted him to come after me. Being chased by a sexy man is a turn on for me. It makes me want to fuck them even harder.

The more time we spent looking each other in the eye, the more I found him attractive. His hands were so soft. He started off reaching in my shorts, stroking my dick slowly. Wow! It was feeling amazing. My dick slowly released pre cum.

I could feel my dick getting slippery with every stroke he took. The moisture fell in between the crevasses of his fingers as he stroked my dick more and more.

In a soft voice I ask him "Shall we?"

I motioned my head towards the back seat then watched him as he crawled on his knees with his ass in the air. We were like two teenage kids laughing while stripping the linen off our backs. Staring at his muscles as he twisted and turned. My tongue developed moisture inside of my mouth. I was ready to implant my teeth gently on his body.

This time around I felt the need to do something different, something wild, I wanted to return home sipping on juice with a mixture of vodka or stretch across my bed thinking about this exact moment. I fell to my knees. I used my strength to push him upward. Crawling under his soft body I carefully held in my hands his weight.

With my tongue stretched all the way out I let his bubble booty fall onto my face. The weight of him, the way his booty cheeks hug my face, I enjoyed the fact I could not breathe. I could feel a soft touch grip around my throbbing dick. He squeezed my ball sack, stroking my dick, then he licked the tip of my dick, where the cum flowed out. His warm mouth fell in love with the way my dick felt inside his mouth. All I could hear was the moans he was accidently letting flow from his vocals.

I don't remember how but we rotated positions a few times. His dick was fat and curvy, not that long, in the range of six inches. My preference is only eight inches and up but the way he wanted me, the way he carried himself, and now a curvy dick was my number one go to. I will divorce my wife right now over a curvy dick. The pulsing inside you when the nut is flowing out the tip, the small manly moans when he hits the right spot or if you're like me and versatile, also when you hit his spot.

My gag reflexes were not the best with guys.

I am more of a top. If I was really into you, I will perform the unexpected, including riding on a hard. throbbing dick. With his dick inside my mouth and down my throat, his hips moving in different directions, he wanted to feel his dick go deep inside my windpipe so I let him go as far as he wanted. With my eyes watering up I could barely make out his facial expressions, but I could see he was loving every moment of his dick inside my windpipe.

In a shaky sexy voice, he said to me "I am about to cum."

I was trying to tell him not to cum in my throat but I was too busy choking. His panting grew louder and faster. My dick was ready to release its cum. I was a far shooter which means the cum would spray onto his body, running down his muscles. I tapped him over and over to let him know I was about to cum.

He said "I am about to cum."

His body tensed up and his moaning got deeper. In a small whisper, moaning, he said

"Tommy." I felt his cum shoot down my throat, his dick pulsing against my teeth. My cum got on his face, lips and hair.

He pulls his dick from my mouth. I ended up swallowing most of his cum. The guy practically made me do that, swallow his cum. That itself turned me on. My dick was getting hard all over again. I quickly opened the car door, coughing up his cum, spitting it out. Seeing a half bottle of water on the car floor, I snatched it as quickly as possible, pouring the warm water inside my mouth and swishing it around.

After drinking some water and spitting the leftovers out, we sat and talked for a small bit of time. The more I looked at him, the more familiar he looked to me. The sex felt almost as if I'd had sex with him before.

I asked the guy "How do you know my name?"

He looked at me and said "I don't know you."

Slowly, I watch a smile form on his face. He was the type of guy that wasn't easy to forget, especially with his smile.

This presence fell on me. I asked him in the most serious voice. In my mind and my heart I knew him. Looking in his eyes, I really wanted to tell him how much I missed him. I was too nervous to say something because I didn't know if he remembered me. Most of our friends at school or our girlfriends had no idea we were in a relationship outside of school. The sex we performed was indescribable, but when he quit the football team and stopped showing up to school, it definitely broke my heart. So many nights I cried while holding the pictures we taken together.

Relaxing back in my seat, I tossed my hands up. I asked him "Man, where have you been?"

While he thought about what he wanted to tell me, I slowly put my underwear back on. He did the same with his, which looked really cute on him.

He asked me "You remember me?"

I nodded my head yes.

He said "Your girlfriend… well, your wife… she came to me in the hallway. She caught me going to the bathroom right before class was over and she said if she saw me, she was going to kill me. The next day my house was broken in to and the new born puppies looked like they were stomped on like a bug."

I replied "So you are saying Kacy did that. I don't know about that. Of course, she had no right talking to you that way."

I could see in his face what he was telling me was true but I could not just not say nothing. He smacked his lips and said to me "My neighbor came to my parents' house and showed us a video of Kacy doing it. Her face was all in the camera. Even though it was so many years ago, I still watch the video every day to remind myself."

His comment intrigued me enough to zoom in even more. I moved forward to the edge of my seat. Leaning forward, I asked him "Remind you of what?"

Before he answered my question we were interrupted by a knock on the window. Sitting there with just our underwear on, sweat rolling down our chests, he looked over at me and said "It is hot in here."

He slowly made a move on me, pressing his lips against my teeth, his tongue rolling around in the inside of my cheeks.

Chapter Seven: Ensnare

When his lips fall into mine it puts me in a beautiful place, enough to fall in love with him. The first day he kissed me, we were in middle school, transitioning into high school. In the middle of being in my own dream I just can't find my lips off his face. Making love with a guy I always found attractive is a dream that has been true. I can hear the window rolling down. I tried to turn my head to look but he placed his hands on my face, making it impossible to look anywhere. I pulled away, looking at him in confusion.

Looking over my shoulder, my eyes could not believe who I was seeing. It was the girl from the gym. She was standing right there, looking right at us. I was speechless. He opened the door and stepped out. Putting his pants on he said "Meet my wife." My jaw disconnected from my face. I had nothing to say. He continued "You should see the look on your face. Oh, wait. Your face is turned upside down because you were fucking her brains out. That is exactly why I married her because I like to watch that ass throwback shots, but I don't like being inside of it like I do yours."

Looking at my old friend I saw something was wrong with him. He leaned inside the car and said "The way Kacy stomped on my puppies will be the same way I step on you both. I will press the weight of your world right on top of you."

He looks at his wife before walking away. His wife tossed in a piece of black paper, folded neatly. I fetched it from the passenger seat. On the front of the note was an emoji and the face on it was laughing. Smacking my lips, I felt like I'd been caught off guard and played like a man at a sex party.

I decided to read the letter later rather than right then. My day was already full of bullshit. I had to see where the hell Kacy was at. I had to get the hell out of this parking lot, but first I had to do something. I quickly jumped out the car, putting on my clothes. I searched the car to make sure there was no evidence for Kacy to find. Placing my gears in reverse, I did not get far before stomping on the breaks.

In the rearview mirror was a guy more than six feet tall and one hundred pounds. He was looking right at me, turning around in my seat while I watched him and wondered what would be next. His body leaning to the side motionless, he looked like his soul was a bargain at a price he forgot to pay. His eyes didn't blink and the skin covering his flesh was thick like an armadillo's.

Pushing my car to its full potential of just over one hundred and fifteen miles an hour with tons of things on my mind, all I could think about was seeing my high school sweetheart. The way he played was a chess play. That was not his first time. I guess the only reason why I felt any emotion about it is because the sex was amazing. I'd cum so hard and I could still feel it coming out.

A very loud 'Stop the car!' rang in my ears.

It felt as if each letter was bouncing off my eardrum. My hands fell off the steering wheel as my car began swerving on the road. I couldn't see or hear, pressing firmly down on the brake pedal. My body jerked and hit my chin on the steering wheel, causing my nose to bleed. Trying to open my eyes, everything had a blurry look to it. A deep, dark voice said in my ear, "Are you looking for me?"

Jumping from my seat, I fell out of my car and onto the concrete, taking a hard impact and causing pain to my shoulder. Laying on my back, I pushed myself away from the car using my two hands. Looking around, I didn't see anyone, just smoke rising from the hood of my car. It smelled like a decomposing body, so I covered my nose with my hand. There was movement in the bushes right behind me. Rushing to my feet, I stood there looking inside my car, but no one was inside.

Seated in the driveway of my house, I tried to settle my nerves by reaching to turn off the car. But I couldn't move. My back was stuck to the seat.

I felt a heavy hand touch my shoulders and my heart started to race, as if I could hear my chest breaking open. Reaching my arms out as far as I could, the stench in the car smelled like something was burning. I began to feel his flesh falling into my lap, peeling from his bones as if it was melting butter.

The demon paralyzed my body, forcing me to watch him. I couldn't blink and the dryness burned my eyes. Screaming was pointless; I had already tried. I stopped fighting and stared directly into the eyes of a lifeless demon. When he opened his mouth, I could hear the voices of all the souls he had taken, the voices screaming "Help! Give me my soul back!" I could hear the flames from his mouth. Even though those voices were dead, the souls could still feel the pain of continuous burning.

I felt my body fall into relaxation after hours of torment as I opened the car door. My body felt as if it was crushed over and over again. I was only steps away from being inside my house and wanted to get inside and fall back onto my soft bed.

Staggering around the corner, I saw Kacy, my wife, standing outside. I wanted to say something, but she didn't look like herself. Her body language was stiff.

Someone was standing with her, smiling and resting their hand on her shoulder. I asked her to turn the porch light on.

"Kacy, Kacy," I repeated her name.

The man with her covered her eyes. In a deep voice, he said, "She is ours now." They both disappeared inside the house, and I began screaming her name. That voice was familiar; it was the same demon that was in the car with me.

Getting through the door of my house, I screamed for Kacy. I was struggling to stand on my two feet, my body was seconds away from falling apart. I walked around the house screaming Kacy's name. I fell into the living room wall and groaned in pain, sliding down the wall and falling to the floor. Right now, all I could think about was getting to the couch. I pulled myself across the floor all the way to the couch and tried to push myself up, but my body had taken a beating today. I just rested right there on the floor of the living room.

Time flew by like freedom as I slept. My eyes were heavy, trying to stay swift gliding across my nose. The smell of roses filled the room. Was I in another dream? Looking around, I noticed I wasn't on the floor. Looking behind me, Kacy was rubbing my back. She said, "I was the one who put you on the couch. No worries," as she rubbed my shoulders.

Kacy handed me a glass of water, and it was right on time. I slurped down the ice-cold water, small pieces of ice sliding down my throat. Every bit of the water inside the glass quenched my thirst. No more than thirty minutes later, I felt reborn all over again. I felt the pores in my skin open up and took a deep breath. I let my head fall back as Kacy went to the room. I closed my eyes, enjoying the fact that I made it home.

I couldn't help but fall into a sleep, even

though I was just waking up. I didn't want to go back to sleep, feeling well-rested enough.

I opened my eyes and there he was, the love of my life, smiling. That was my favorite part about him. He leaned over, kissing me. I love how you can kiss someone you love and open your eyes and see their face pressing against yours. That is what I did - I opened my eyes to see him against me. Instead, I was looking at the demon that was in the back seat of my car, trying to take my soul from me. The moment I tried to scream, he began choking me. I was kicking and swinging my hands, and he leaned upward. The skin from his body melted, falling on my face, and the skin falling inside my mouth. He said to me, "You are a part of me now."

Falling onto the floor, I tried to scramble to safety. The wood floor below my palms moved like waves in the ocean. The more I tried to crawl to safety, the worse the waves moved, making safety impossible. The demon stood in the corner, laughing. I began to scream "Stop!" continuously. I must have pissed this demon off because he began slowly moving towards me.

The wood floor stopped moving like the ocean waves. My body was pinned down to the floor as the demon stood over me. A loud roar and cries of many voices scattered the atmosphere. His long, sharp fingers started snatching off his melting, burning skin. Under the skin were many faces screaming for help. His body began to grow new skin - cleaner, healthier skin, white skin.

Looking up into his eyes, the only words that could leave my mouth were 'holy shit.' I looked at a smile I fell in love with many years ago. The lips that drowned me in a fantasy, the same eyes that I could never look away from the very first day he stepped into our school many years ago. The same skin I felt rubbing against mine, the same exact man I loved more than my wife.

Chapter Eight: A Purpose Behind Every Decision

Slowly taking one step at a time, I walked around the corner and watched Tommy suffer from the mistakes his father made. I was too busy doing my own thing, trying to figure out how to open the small box from the dungeon. But I needed peace and quiet, and the noise was too much. You can only get to a demon by speaking their language, called Bellsybabble. I learned it while I was in the dungeon of the church. I asked the demon to leave the killing up to me.

Disappearing back into my room, I stood looking at the beautiful box, wondering why it wouldn't open. Looking over my shoulder, I could hear the water running in the kitchen. That's what sparked the idea that Tommy might be the only one who could open this box. That was the only explanation. Thinking about it, he was the one who inherited everything. I picked up the box and carried it to the kitchen, setting it down on the counter. Tommy turned around and asked me, "What is that?"

I smiled and replied, 'This box was your father's, now it is yours, and only you can open it.' Tommy walked up to the box, twisting it around and looking at the dimensions. Tommy said, 'My father always said to me that the best hiding places are in plain sight.' I rested my ass on the counter, sitting right next to the box. Tommy turned the box over, and I was trying to see what he was messing with.

His hands were too big for me to see, but he disconnected the bottom from the box. He lifted the box in the air and said in a smooth voice, "Just because it has an entrance doesn't mean that is the way." There was an old piece of paper sticking up, so I reached over and retrieved the paper from the box. Tommy's eyes followed my hand as I pulled the folded paper to me.

Unfolding it, the first thing I saw was some

numbers. It almost looked like an old check.

Unfolding it quickly, Tommy snatched the old check from my hand and said to me in a shocking voice, "Seventy-five thousand dollars!"

Tommy looked at me, and I looked back at him. Out of curiosity, I asked, "Will they cash this check? It is overdue. Tommy, the check was made out in 1724." He waited, and then said, "There is a note."

Tommy retrieved the note from the box and slowly opened it. I could tell he was nervous about what it was going to say. The note said, 'If you found this letter, then you must be my son. And if you figured out my hidden place, then you will find more. Getting this far, I can only imagine what you have been through. If you decide to do exactly what I say, you will be very rich in the next 48 hours. I must warn you that with great financial freedom comes a great debt. Take this to the bank. The directions are on the back.'

Looking over at Tommy, I knew exactly

what his father was talking about. I just wondered if Tommy understood. We turned the letter over, and there it was - all the information we needed and the name of the person we needed to talk to.

The very next morning was quiet. I'm guessing everyone was inside their heads. To open the air, I started off by asking Tommy what was on his mind. He shrugged his shoulders and was playing the quiet game. Okay, so be it. I just knew we had money to get our hands on, and I didn't care what came with it. I want it all.

After hours on the road, I was getting a bit hungry. I knew I should have eaten this morning. Listening to the navigation system, we were only a couple of minutes away. Sitting up in my chair, I think I saw the bank from the road. It was shaped like a dome. Getting closer, the architect made it all glass. The structure was outrageously poetic. I fell in love the moment I saw it. Tommy stayed quiet, so I asked him one last time, "Tommy, why are you not saying anything?"

In the calmest voice I had ever heard come from his mouth, he replied, "I am hoping this money buys us freedom." Looking at Tommy, I wanted to ask more, but right now, this money would be the only escape from sleeping next to him at night. What is his is mine, and what is mine is not his, unless he was willing to die for it. Being polite, I held open the glass double doors for Tommy. Tommy stood in the middle of the door, one foot inside the bank and one foot outside. He turned, facing me, and said, "I know what you said to my friend all those years ago. Your evil way drove him to quit school and the football team."

Why couldn't he keep his comment to himself? I enjoyed it more when he wasn't saying a word. I walked right in front of Tommy, cutting him off and leaving him to hold the door. But I couldn't let him get the last word. I replied to his comment, "You miss him?" Walking up to Tommy and standing toe to toe with him, I continued, "If you don't stop, he will be missing you. Now can we go get this money?" Me and Tommy put on smiles and we continued to the bank teller.

An older lady walks from her office, making her way to us. Leading with a bright white smile, short blond curly hair, and I could see her nipples. In a loud, exciting voice, she said, "Hi, welcome to Hell Bank!" We nodded, accepting her welcome, and she continued, "Right this way." This was the final moment to see what Tommy's dad was really worth. Walking into her office, the energy was complicated. I felt it before, stuck below the church.

In an excited voice, the lady asks, "What do you have for me today?"

Tommy handed her the check, and we both looked at her, waiting for her reaction.

She made eye contact with both of us and said, "I will get the right person in here. Just know she has been waiting for you, Mr. Grey."

The clerk made her way to the exit. Right before she walked out, I watched her graze against

Tommy's shoulder. That made my day and aroused my pussy to be warm. It was hot watching him get hit on.

I told Tommy I saw what the clerk did and I let him know I enjoyed it. We shared a small laugh. The door opened behind us, but no one came in. We turned around and standing there was an old, fragile lady with short white hair. She said, "Come with me." Before we had a chance to stand up, the old lady walked off, leaving us behind. We had to play the catch-up game.

Following behind her, we went through double doors into her office. The inside of the office had portraits of old Greek gods and dragons, and the windows were all black. The energy in the room was evil and corrupted. We sat in chairs with bone armrests. The old lady had dull, coffee-stained teeth and a look in her eye that made me uneasy. Who was this old lady?

She looked up at me and, in a slow voice, said "I see you met the serpent."

She slowly stood up from her chair and walked towards Tommy, leaning in to whisper something in his ear. I could see Tommy's neck veins start to swell as she whispered to him. The lady looked over Tommy's shoulder directly at me and said "I know who you are." She walked back to her seat, leaning back and smiling. We all sat there looking at each other before anything was said, but then she said "Only a small group of people had checks like this one."

She held the check up in the air and continued, "Almost all of us are dead; some were murdered, and for the others, people were too weak to continue our legacy. And Tommy here," she pointed right at Tommy, "his father was our last generation. The only difference is that Tommy's father was our only black slave. He was special to all of us, until he couldn't pay his debt. And I see why, to leave it to his son."

Tommy pulled me close to him, tucking me under his shoulders. The older lady leaned close to her desk and whispered, "You are being watched."

I leaned back into my seat, as did Tommy. This old bitch has more power than God, but I had more power than a human's life.

I replied to her comment, "Well, this check better be worth my time."

The old lady replied, "Grey is a family name. Do not ever forget that." She pointed at me and continued, "What is given can be taketh."

I look over at my husband, who sits there looking like a scary bitch. The old lady stands from her seat and pulls a soft chair next to Tommy. She says, "Tommy, before we move any further, a word was passed on to me to give to you. I was told to tell you that I love you. Those words are from your father's mouth." Whatever the old lady said made Tommy sit forward in his chair.

Tommy replied, "Wait, you know my father?" The old lady laughed and giggled. She said, "Son, I was the one who gave your father the opportunity. And that opportunity is the only reason why you're sitting next to me in my office right now, today. I had to look after you most of your life." Tommy stood up and walked around the room, covering his mouth with one hand. The old lady continued, "Your father was a powerful man. His only mistake was that he refused to hold up his end of the deal."

Sitting back and watching all of this unfold was the perfect opportunity for me to gather the information I needed to make sure my carefully crafted blueprint went through.

The old lady said to Tommy with a smile on her face, "Mr. Grey, you are now worth one hundred million dollars."

When those words came out of her mouth, my mouth dropped open in shock. Tommy finally relaxed, leaning back in his chair.

I stood up from my chair, stretching my limbs until I felt something pop. It felt like I grew a few inches. It had all been interesting, but I had been sitting in that chair for too long. The old lady stood up and went back to her seat, gasping as she leaned back in her soft chair. She said to Tommy, "What you just inherited is a slave's inheritance, and you are his son. Enjoy it, but just remember that everything comes with a price. Just remember something for me."

The old lady stood up and handed Tommy a check with a pen on top of it. She continued, "Remember what your dad taught you: the most well-hidden places are in plain sight." After Tommy signed the check, we made an exit out of the office. The old lady said, "Wait, wait, Tommy. I have something for you, and in time your eyes only should see." The old lady reached into her desk and pulled out a black envelope with "from dad" written on the front.

The old lady gave us specific instructions for bringing the check back to Hell's Bank to cash it. The clerk behind the counter had long orange hair pulled back in a ponytail, was tall, and had a caramel color. She said that sixty million dollars would be available in the next fifteen minutes, with a twenty-five-minute maximum. The additional forty million would become available within the next seventy-two hours. She handed us both debit cards and we requested that four million dollars be held in a bond account.

The drive home was amazing. Tommy was exciting. He reached over and started off rubbing my leg. Biting my bottom lip, in a slow, soft voice I asked him "You want to go deeper?"

He looked at me and smiled. I quickly unzipped my pants, pulling my pants down right along with my blue thong that was up my pussy. Tommy slid his hand across my soft skin and placed his index finger on my clit.

Rubbing it, I began panting as he continued to rub my clit at a rapid pace. Moaning, I told him "Faster, faster. If you want my pussy to cum, go faster... harder."

Tommy pulled the car over. He leaned over my seat, placing his head between my thighs, sticking his tongue inside my pussy.

"Tommy, I'm about to cum!"

He began rubbing faster, harder with his tongue and fingers.

"I am about to cum, ahhhhh!"

My pussy started spitting out cum, Tommy lips slurping it all out, my body jerking.

I could not take it anymore. I pushed Tommy's head away. He started laughing, put the car into drive and we went off down the road.

We were not even ten minutes inside the house and he was already screaming he was tired. My pussy had cum all over it. A bitch needed to step in the shower. My face under the water, I scrubbed my face with face scrub and I thought I heard something. Pulling my face from the water, I listened… but there was nothing.

Sitting on the corner of the bed wearing a see-through candy green thong and a matching candy green bra, I took my time shuffling through the photos I found under the church. After going through every picture, I noticed the same exact white man was in each one with Tommy's father. It could have been his best friend but what if it was not? Who was this white man?

Closing my eyes, I tried desperately to remember the visions the demons allowed me to see inside the dungeon of the church. I remembered seeing his face but I just couldn't make it out. My vision was getting blurry and I smacked my lips in frustration.

Wait a second...

I turned all the photos over and just as I thought, each photo had names on the back: Al Mammon, Asmodeus, Leviathan, Beelzebub, Belphegor, Centaur, Griffin, Stolas, and Paimon.

Chapter Nine: Hidden in Plain Sight

I found out Tommy's father's name was Clauneck Grey. Putting together a puzzle with lost pieces is the most complicated task in the world. I told myself I could do it and collected all the pictures with Clauneck Grey's name on the back. Then I placed all the pictures in one pile with Clauneck and the white boy, which was almost all of the pictures.

After my elimination process, I was down to five photos and still had no name for Clauneck Grey's best friend. Frustrated, I tossed the photos against the wall. I don't know why I was so dedicated to finding out who this white guy was. Allowing my skin to stick to the sheets, my body fell deep into the softness of the bed. Suddenly, something was itching the shit out of my back. Reaching under me, it felt like a piece of paper. Sitting up, I found a photo I had never seen before. And there it was - the name of Clauneck's best friend, Mictian.

I found what I was looking for but I still could not wrap my mind around why Clauneck Grey was smiling in every picture with white people. In his time, slavery was at its peak. Sliding down to the floor with my legs crossed, I leant my head in the palm of my hands, fingers tapping the side of my face, pondering. Then I went back to when I was trapped inside the dungeon under the church. The eyes that snake looked at me with made me horny.

Moisture developing between my thighs, my nipples getting hard, my head fell backwards. My hand reached for my nipples, squeezing them harder and harder. My other hand quickly went between my legs, softly touching the outer side of my clit. I twitched. I'd never felt this horny and I'd never felt this good touching myself. I gripped my whole entire titty. My tongue felt light.

Opening my mouth wide and stretching my tongue until the tip was touching my nipples, my fingers finding their way inside my pussy, thrusting my fingers, pushing in and out. A different feeling was coming up my spine. I'd never felt so much energy before. My tongue stretched down lower and lower. I could never do this before - my tongue had a mind of its own, sliding inside of me, going deeper than I could ever imagine.

Finally, I found the strength to open my eyes. Wait a second, looking down in confusion, I don't remember a mirror. I am lying inside of a pentagram. I quickly jump up on my feet, tossing on my clothes, and rushing to the front room.

Where the fuck is Tommy?

Walking through the house, he was not there.

Someone is playing games with me.

I stopped, put my hands on my lips, and just remembered. I went to the bathroom, opened my mouth, and stuck out my tongue. My tongue was split down the middle and could stretch to the floor.

Looking down into the sink, I was still trying to calm down. Having to slurp my tongue back into my mouth did not make the thought of it any better. I knew I had to clear my head.

Wrapping my fingers around the ice-cold water bottle, taking it from the fridge, the moisture sent a refreshing feeling through my body. Taking a deep breath, closing my eyes, tipping the bottle, placing the ridges on the tip of my teeth, the water flowed to the tip of my tongue, flowing across my taste buds. It was so refreshing.

A sound from the inside of the house caused me to drop the bottle onto the floor. Sitting there just for a brief second looking at my cold-water flow from the container, I shouted "Oh shit."

I took off running to the bathroom, taking my favorite cherry red bath towel from the towel holder. I ran back into the kitchen and began to clean up my mess.

Some of the water splashed onto the lingerie I was wearing. I could not walk around like this. While the water soaks up, I will be in my room changing my sex attire. Even though I really did not want to wear my neon orange see through thong and bra, until my clothes were finished drying, that was what I'd be wearing, plus it looks good on my soft, cinnamon shade, skin tone.

On my knees, drying up the spilled water, my imagination began to run wild. I could feel a strong girl walk into the kitchen and telling me to crawl on the floor. Imagining her walking up to me with her big black dildo swinging between her legs, she walks up to me and forces me to spit on the dick. With my ass up and pussy wet, ready to be taken advantage of, punishing me for making a mess in the kitchen.

While in my fantasy on my knees in the kitchen, I thought I heard a text on someone's phone. I wanted to ignore it because I knew my fantasy was going to lead to me having sex with myself with a glass dildo. Pushing myself from the floor, I walked back to the bedroom, taking my time to check to see if it was my phone. Then I heard it again. Slowly, I made my way to the front door. As soon as I pulled the front door open, I should have known it. It was Tommy's black ass texting.

I ask him "What the hell are you doing?" with my hands on my hips.

He replied "Nothing."

That is the shit I hate when they say nothing but they be physically doing something.

I left him right where I found him, on the concrete at the door. Tommy began following me.

"What have I done to you?" he screamed.

Facing Tommy, I replied "The question is, what haven't you done?"

I moved Tommy aside and went into the bathroom, closing him out. Standing in the mirror and facing my reflection, I felt like a demon facing a God. That thing in the dungeon did this to me.

The female behind the mirror is not the woman that was pushed out her momma's pussy, and the female standing looking into the mirror, she has a dark side, ready for anything. And now we are one hundred million dollars richer.

It was almost time to end this excitement. It was time to kill my husband.

Right then, I could use some fresh air. If Tommy said anything to me, I would trick him into having sex, then bite down on his dick and take it off.

Slowly, walking through the living room, I glanced over at him. He was on the couch, asleep. That sorry son of a bitch went out to find sex. But I wonder who it was this time, a boy or a whore. Everyone knew Tommy. He can be either a bitch or a man at any moment.

Chapter Ten: The Missing Piece of the Puzzle

Walking up behind Tommy, I slapped him on the head and screamed, 'Wake up! Tommy, fill me in on something: where did your father get all this money, and why haven't I heard about this?' Tommy scooted his butt up on the couch, looking sideways at me. He responded, 'What the hell are you talking about?' His stupid comment forced me to throw my purse on the couch.

Looking him right in the eyes, I used my finger to direct him to move closer. Tommy looked at me nervously. Slowly, I opened my mouth. My bones popped, my jawbone dislocated, and the split in my tongue rose from my mouth. My jawbone continued to stretch as the split of my tongue floated from the bottom of my mouth and slowly slithered to Tommy's lips, entering his mouth.

Tommy was stuck in shock as I walked up behind him and slapped him on the head, screaming "Wake up, Tommy. Fill me in on something: where did your father get all this money, and why haven't I heard about this?" Tommy scooted his butt up on the couch and looked sideways at me, responding with a confused "What the hell are you talking about?" His stupid comment forced me to throw my purse on the couch and stare him in the eyes with a pointed finger, directing him to move forward.

Tommy looked at me nervously as I slowly opened my mouth and bones popped, my jaw bone dislocating as the split of my tongue rose from my mouth. My jaw bone still stretched as the split of my tongue floated from the bottom of my mouth and slowly slithered towards Tommy's lips, entering into his mouth. I could feel his manhood shatter into dust as I took control, the adrenaline rushing through my skin and coldness flushing through my veins. I saw my reflection in Tommy's eyes as my eye color turned the same color as the snake eyes I saw in the dungeon below the church.

As I tapped into their bloodline, I began to slowly see everything – the reenactment played out right in front of me, with tables and chairs coming from above. I was in the middle of the torture and sacrifices that the slaves had to endure. Their young were eaten alive. Clauneck, Tommy's father, was the one who started the entire organization and introduced it to the white people. He was the breeder for all the girls, with the goal of getting as many people with his bloodline as possible. After the girls had babies, Clauneck would throw a feast, cooking the girls whole and stuffing the empty insides of their stomachs with vegetables.

Bouncing to another vision, looking around, this vision was right behind the church. This must have been when Clauneck Grey gave his soul to the devil. Satan and Clauneck Grey bargain with each other. Satan asks Clauneck to tell his friends to join him in a feast, Satan placing a stack of body limbs in the middle of a pentagon. Everyone was laughing, drinking, and having sex.

None of Clauneck Grey's friends asked what the feast was for, but Satan and Clauneck had different plans. It was to kill everyone. This was Clauneck's first sacrifice. He had to kill everyone he loved. The first sacrifice granted him freedom and put him in a position to be in charge. The second sacrifice was to give his mind to Satan. Satan wanted to be fully in control.

Clauneck Grey would inherit wealth and a son, but what Satan didn't know was that Clauneck Grey negotiated a deal with a witch. She cast a spell that would reverse the deal at a certain time, certain year, and at a certain hour. Clauneck Grey would have to die early for the spell to work. The witch warned Clauneck Grey that if he decided to go through with this, Satan would find out and bring wrath, pain, backstabbing, lust, and death among his entire generation for eternity.

It was time for an upgrade, so later that night I called a realtor to help us look for a mansion. I wanted something with an open floor plan, wooden panels throughout the house, and 16 bedrooms with an equal number of bathrooms. I also wanted two pools and two hot tubs. A palace was on my wish list and I wanted to be seated at the throne. This opportunity was exactly what I had been waiting for.

I don't mind dating a demon's son if it means getting one hundred million dollars into my bank account. Soon I'll have to meet the realtor, but right now I'm not ready for that. A good jog through my new neighborhood is the best way for a rich woman like me to relieve stress and see who I might fuck. Hmm, maybe I go hunting for some fat, juicy, hard dick but also my mouth was also in the mood for a fat, puffy, tight, squirting pussy, so I got into my sex closet and slid on my running joggers with no thong and my favorite high yellow sports bra. I tied my hair in a pony tail, turned my music loud and my body felt excited.

I was already sweaty a few miles into the jog. The air felt different, lighter and cleaner. A guy was also jogging in front of me. His ass was fat.

I sped up and fairly soon we were running side by side. Looking over at him, I saw he was ugly but his body was in extremely good shape. Looking down between the running man legs, I saw his dick was curvy and hitting the side of his legs.

The running man was definitely a grower and a shower. I tapped him on his shoulder and showed him my beautiful smile. The running man looked down at my titties. I nodded at him to follow me. I took him on an adventure then we stopped behind a tall tree. The running man pushed me against the tree and then he jumped inside my mouth. I pulled away. Kissing strangers was not my thing. I reached between his legs, squeezing his hard dick. Turning around with my ass against his ball sack, he turned me back around, pulling my leggings down.

His hard curvy dick jumping out of his running shorts, I began slapping my pussy with two of my fingers, getting my pussy extremely wet. I did not have that much time.

I told him "Shove that curvy dick inside me."

The running man wrapped his hand around my throat and shoved his hard throbbing, pre-cumming wet dick inside me. I almost started screaming from how good it felt.

His dick's head was round and pressing against the inner walls of my wet, fat, tight pussy. He was squeezing my throat extremely hard. I could barely breathe. The running man was still shoving his curvy, hard dick inside of me. My pussy was about to squirt and cum at the same time. My eyes rolled to the back of my head and my tongue was hanging from my mouth. I heard him say "Oh shit!" and I squirted and cum all over his dick.

I could feel his dick throbbing inside of me, the cum spraying deep inside of me. When he pulled his dick out I could feel more of his cum spray on my pussy lips. He still had a hold of my throat. The running man pulled my neck forward, kissed me on my forehead and dropped me on the ground. Before he disappeared in the distance, he said to me "That pussy was the best pussy I ever put my dick inside."

While Kacy was running around, I was up doing my thing. That bitch thought I was asleep. Kacy was after something. The snake in my father's dungeon granted her power and the only way that could have happened was if she'd made a deal, and if she did either it was my life on the line or someone she loves. My father, Clauneck Grey, prepared me for these decisions and honestly being this powerful felt right, like I belonged in the position. Before I plan her death, she must have my child. That was the only way to break the generational curse.

At the time I was so young and confused by what my grandmother told me. As I got older and smarter, I began hearing voices in my head guiding me through certain situations. In the middle of the night I would look in the mirror and see different faces.

Kacy had no idea I'd been watching her since high school. She was the one I had to get married to, and at a specific time, she would have to have my baby. She was chosen by Satan.

The only reason Kacy made it out alive is because it wasn't in the plan for her to die or be in the dungeon. When I lie next to her at night, I can feel her soul slowly being pulled from her body. I beg the demons and gods to let her live just until the ritual is complete. Like my father,, I am good at borrowing time. I negotiate a deal with Satan for her to live until it's the right time to hand her over for the sacrifice.

However, when the snake bit her, it delivered her great power, which was the only way for her to survive. That snake was my father, Clauneck Grey. It was his last wish to the witch to let him live on Earth as a serpent, guarding his temple. The witch warned him she would have to take his sight, but Clauneck agreed. He knew he would see through sound and fear in the human veins.

When the snake injected its venom into Kacy's body, it took effect on her within seconds, numbing her body and shutting down her system. It also forced her brain into hallucinations, confusion, and the sensation of death. When Kacy removed the box from the dungeon, Satan was enraged and Clauneck Grey became angry. Her actions caused her to open a door that was meant to remain closed until the next generation.

When I was approached by the man with burning skin, the many souls I heard screaming also told me to kill Kacy and offer her to the demons in the pentagon for them to feast on. Divorcing her would put me in a position to finally marry a sexy man. I want him to have a nice, slim, round butt, a toned body, a little body hair, and a curvy dick.

Chapter Eleven: I Carved Out the Navel

The gym was my favorite place to be. The women were sexy and their husbands and boyfriends didn't seem to be satisfying them much. Most of the sexy moms practically lived in the gym. And the men had slim, nice bubble butts. When I first started taking my body seriously, I used to run into the bathroom, pull out my hard dick, and start masturbating, leaving cum on the sink and floor.

When you're in a place with highly sexual people, you never know what the outcome might be or when you might have sex. Everyone at the gym definitely knew there was zero chance of that happening while you were taking a number two. Some people did it anyway, then they came out with sweat sliding between their legs and in their ass cracks. It was a disgusting thought. I've been going to this gym for a long time now and I still can't find a guy who's worthy enough to touch my athletic body or be inside my athletic bubble butt.

I might have arrived too soon. It seems like a lot of people are staying home today; the way the scenery is set up there will not be much attention for me to embrace. So, I decided to start my morning in the private workout room. It's smaller, but the weights did their job. The muscles in my forearms have been aching for two days in a row, I had to loosen up. My bones felt stiff, my joints needed to stretch. I stepped on the treadmill, it started off slowly, gradually picking up speed, I was determined to keep this body in shape.

Drip after drip, I began to sweat, the salty sweat running down my chest, the moisture gathering on my skin cooled me down. My lungs were fighting for air, but I wouldn't stop. My legs were getting tired, but I couldn't stop. There wasn't enough pain for me to give up. An hour went by and my body felt broken, tired, I was fighting to hold on. Having people around you makes it a bit easier, I couldn't show people my weakness.

Next, I moved on to the bench press. My

body was feeling energized today, and I had one more mile to go before I was done. I wasn't paying attention to who walked into the room, but I noticed someone out of the corner of my eye. I heard the door close and I had just thirty more seconds left on my workout. I counted down: ten, nine, eight, seven, six, five, four, three, two, one.

Running alongside me was a cute guy - muscular, chocolate-skinned, handsome, and my personal favorite - well-endowed. The sight of his sparkling body sent me straight to heaven. By the time my eyes unglued from his dick, the man was already looking at me.

He said, "You like what you see?"

With a gentle smile, I couldn't keep my eyes off him and replied, "Only if I can have what I see."

My eyes went back to his penis as the man started to pulse it.

I have an idea. I cut my treadmill run short and moved to the bench press. I put on 350 pounds while the man was still running.

I asked him, "Will you spot me?"

He replied, "Of course I will, only if you spot me as well. This looks like some good weight to do a few reps with."

I thought to myself that we would be fucking in a few minutes. After a few reps, I just lay there resting my arms.

Looking up, I can see his dick pushed to the side. It looks so scrumptious and the head of his dick is looking right back at me. I wish the cum would spray all over my face.

Out of nowhere, the man said to me, "Get it if you want it."

My hands slowly go up his leg and into his shorts, and there it was - my hands wrap around his big, hard monster dick. Placing his nuts inside the palm of my hand, it never felt so comforting and nice. The man caressed my head, sliding his fingers through my hair as he leaned across the weight bar to kiss me. I continued to play with his dick, holding his nuts as he thrust forward, pushing his dick inside my throat. The man's aggressiveness turned me on. He pulled his dick out of my throat and in a deep, manly voice told me to turn over and arch my back so he could watch my ass jiggle. A guy like this is rare; he's straight, beats on his wife, and when he's angry, his muscles in his throat flare up.

While he was busy crawling on top of me, I could feel his hard dick sliding up my body. He is crawling on top of me. I lift my ass up, his face pushing between my thighs, my lungs behind my rib cage, inhaling and exhaling. His tongue was moving around inside of me while my tongue fell from my mouth. My dick was hard as a rock. The man stroked his hard dick in my tight ass. I was on the edge of cumming.

In silence I was crying for his dick. The man smacked my ass as hard as he could.

"Look at that fat bubble," the man said in a deep voice.

He had taken both of my legs, spreading my

thighs so that my asshole was touching the weight bench. I did everything he asked me to do. Not looking into his eyes, everything I wanted to see was in the mirror. He had me, a virgin.

My body was ready to give up. This man has sprayed cum inside me twice already. I sprayed my cum backwards three times. He takes his hands, squeezing them around my waist tightly as he is thrusting his hard, thick, wet dick inside of my stomach. My body became numb, my feet tingled, my fingers tensing up, my asshole jumping, and my imagination escaping from me. I didn't know if I could hang on until he cum inside me again.

"Get it over with, already!" I moaned.

"Shut up!" he replied.

The man spits all over my asshole. I'd never had that done to me before but I liked it. It sent butterflies through my entire body. Gasping for air, it felt like his dick was growing bigger. The man was going deeper, deeper, and deeper inside me.

"I'm getting close, oh man," the guy moans.

He reaches around, putting my hard, throbbing dick in the palm of his hands.

He began jacking me off and he said "Can we cum at the same time?"

The feeling was beyond any feeling I'd ever felt, like my entire body was shrinking in his hand.

The guy moans "I'm cumming, ah!"

I followed right behind him.

I moan "I am about to cum!"

I can feel his dick releasing his cum inside of me and my dick was throbbing in his hand. His body leaned on top of me, his chest resting on my back. My body went forward, my stomach flat on the bench.

I saw him look at his watch.

He said to me, "I think I have to go."

I smiled and shook my head okay. He rushed out the door as I sat there and watched him. Before he left, I should have told him I wanted some more dick, this time in a different position, but he was already gone. I sighed while pushing myself up. One by one, I put on my clothes. Finally fully dressed, I sat there thinking about if I wanted to go home and deal with that crazy bitch, Kacy, or stay and finish my work out.

I decided to stay and work out.

Laying on my back and gripping the iron above my head, positioning myself to push the weight off the rail, I had trouble because I could not stop thinking about the man that had just left. Finally, I pushed the iron off, knocking out ten reps. I sat, wiggled my arms loose, then continued to strive through ten more reps. I continued a few more reps on the bench press. After ten more reps my body began to tingle, acting kind of weird. As I was sitting there I kind of felt like I had to fart. No big deal. I pushed and nothing came out.

My stomach was still bothering me so I pushed one last time. I rushed to the men's restroom. Not going to lie, that was the best shit I had ever taken. Pushing out that guy's cum felt different and very loud. On my way out of the men's restroom I felt better and horny. I needed to put my cum in someone's guts, besides Kacy's. Something soft, tight, and a voice that bites back.

It was past time for me to get home. I patiently waited for a female to compliment me. Walking around the gym with my hands in my sweater pocket, after a few minutes I saw a girl standing at the corner, texting on her phone. She stood tall, skinny, sexy, and I could tell her pussy is fresh. Watching her, studying her, her manner was adult but her face looked young. The girl stayed looking at her phone but not once did she look up. As a grown man, I approached her. I am so used to females approaching me and it made my game easier if a female approaches first.

I made my move on her. We started exchanging words and this led to laughs. Then, at the right moment, I leaned on her lips. Her lips were extremely soft and tasted amazing. I could feel my dick growing. My dick became extremely hard. I was prepared to fuck this hoe in the hallway. She lightly placed her hand on my chest. Her nails were painted cherry red. Pushing myself back from her mouth, I looked at her bright brown eyes.

Reaching around to get a handful of her ass while I ground my dick against her long legs, I wanted to cum so hard inside her guts before I stuck my hard dick inside her booty. The girl grabbed a handful of my nuts. She gently rolled them in her hands. It felt so amazing, it had me standing on my toes.

"Bark like a dog," she demanded.

I began to bark like a dog. This girl had my nut in her hands so I was going to do anything she asked of me.

The girl slid down on her knees, taking my pants down with her. She slapped my dick on her face and lips. I watched my dick bounce off her soft lips and skin. While she was looking up at me from her knees, she opened her mouth and slowly placed my dick inside it. Her mouth was warm as an oven. She started to push my dick down her tiny throat. If it did not go down easily, she forced it too - her gag reflex was top of the line.

It felt so pleasurable for my hard throbbing dick to be in her throat. I snatched a handful of her hair. Pulling her head backwards, I repositioned us by throwing my legs over her shoulders. I decided to bend her backwards until she could not bend anymore, with my dick going straight down her throat, past the tonsils. She gagged and spit, getting my dick even more wet. Her hand squeezes my ball sack.

Her reflexes were amazing, definitely a pro. In that case, she has had her mouth on too many dicks. The girl pulls away from almost dying by a dick in her throat. Standing on her feet, she leans on the wall with her ass out, shaking her nice small round fat ass. My dick was so hard, I could feel the cum already wanting to slowly burst out of it. I jammed my throbbing dick inside her. She screamed and tried to move. It was such a turn on.

Her ass was bouncing as I was stroking from

the back, the best back shots I ever had. As her ass threw back, I leaned forward, pinching her nipples. Her moans were small. I was dying to hear her scream. I pinched her nipples really hard, then harder. I thrusted harder, getting rougher with her, slapping her across the face. My plan with her was to take all my anger out on her pussy and to put her body in a whole lot of pain.

Chapter Twelve: Stick to the Blueprint

"Get on your knees, bitch," I demanded.

Wrapping her hair around my hand and snatching her body to her knees, the noises she made were exactly what I had been waiting for. Pressing my big dick against her lips until my dick fell on top of her tongue, rubbing my ball sack on her chin, in a soft voice she said to me "Nut, daddy."

Taking my dick from her mouth, I masturbated in front of her face. The strokes felt good. I was so close, my legs began to shake, my body jerking.

I said to the girl "I am about to cum."

My cum sprayed all over her face and hair.

I was surprised we actually fucked in the gym hallway. That is the only benefit of not a lot of people being here. The girl told me a little about herself as we put on our clothes. She was an office assistance, had graduated college, and was going back for her masters. And she loved squirrels.

We were both finishing getting dressed. I smiled at her and she said to me "I had a good time" as she smiled back.

I asked her "Would you mind walking with me to my car?"

She walked up to me and embraced me with a hug.

"Sure, let's go."

Half way to my car the girl let go of my hand. I asked her "What are you doing?"

She pointed. I looked and a shovel hit me in the face, knocking me smooth out.

My vision was blurry, my head hurt, and then I heard a familiar voice. I struggled to look around but I was tied up.

Tommy had no idea I set him up. The girl he was having an affair with was my girlfriend for many years. The only reason why we fell apart was the same reason why Tommy stopped messing with that boy - being married to a female was not a part of my agenda. We still messed around here and there.

Looking at Tommy on the ground tied up like a hog was bringing me great joy. I asked him "You thought you could get away with this?"

A long time ago she was the very first person to touch my pussy, and she was also the first girl to cheat on me with a guy I really liked. That man is now my husband. I knew one day I could use her for something, and give her a taste of her own medicine. Gripping the shovel tight with my hands, with a loud roar the shovel smacked her in the temple, sending the girl straight to the ground.

With no remorse, I beat the girl over and over until the blood start gushing out. I pulled the bitch by her hair, dragging her across the concrete, throwing her body in the back of my trunk.

Walking back to Tommy, I asked him a simple question.

"Bitch, you want to live or die?"

He replied "I want to live."

His voice was a bit shaky.

I replied with vengeance in my voice "Then you will do a sexual favor for me."

I gave Tommy simple directions. I told him to meet me in the bathroom with a girl.

"Draw her to you, then offer her one million dollars to have sex with your wife."

When Tommy went inside, I followed right behind him. He went one direction and I went the opposite direction. I began pacing back and forth, coming up with a plan to kill Tommy. I needed him out my way. He did not deserve to have this money.

The bathroom door slowly opened. The girl was young - between nineteen and twenty-one. She was perfect. She walked into the bathroom alone.

In a soft voice she asks "Is this where I am supposed to be?"

I replied "Only if you want to be here. Did my husband tell you how much money you will make?"

She nodded her head yes.

I was wearing a one- piece skirt, with no panties. I slowly started pulling my skirt up while looking at the girl in her eyes. She was busy looking at my body. She was hypnotized by everything she saw. This girl had already had sex with other females. Sliding down the wall, I sat down on the floor. Slowly opening my legs, the girl crawled to me as I watched her. I closed my eyes. I began praying silently to the devil Gods, offering them a human sacrifice.

Her face pushed between my thighs. I could feel her lips press against my pussy, her tongue swirling around in a circle motion, licking my clit. She knew exactly what she was doing. Leaning my head against the wall, I began to moan. The girl's face pressed harder against my pussy, her tongue going inside of me, licking faster and faster. I moved us in the middle of the floor.

The bathroom door opened up. Tommy stumbled inside the bathroom. The girl attempted to look up but I squeezed her head in between my thighs. Tommy began drawing a circle around us, while holding the side of his ribs. I gently put my hand on her head. I told her I was close to cumming. My body jerked and my pussy released, squirting all in her mouth, giving her a mouthful of pussy juice. My intentions were to be greedy and get as much as I could out of her. This young bitch was going to die tonight. Tommy needed her soul, and I did as well.

The girl could sure eat some pussy. Tommy snatched her up and she hit her head on the wall. She began to scream and fight. I grabbed the black chalk, rushing to finish the pentagram. Tommy slung the girl on the ground, busting her lip. Binding the girl's hands and feet, Tommy stripped his clothes off, getting on top of her. This little young bitch did not think any of this was going to happen to her. She just wanted to make her money.

Tommy forcefully stuck his dick inside of her tiny little pussy. She screamed at the top of her lungs. The girl's titties were small but firm. I watch Tommy squeeze them, Tommy fucking her anyway he wants. I really hated watching this. For some reason, I was horny watching. And the simple fact was I was not getting any of this at home. I held my temper, I had to stick to the blueprint.

He sprayed his cum all in her tight little pussy. Listening to him moan and watching his facial expressions was fucked up, but I also had to remind myself this bitch was worthless.

I took out the knife I carry with me twenty-four seven. I stuck it right where I wanted. I jabbed the knife hard into her stomach. I pulled the knife all the way diagonally across her stomach until I reached the hip bone. The girl's eyes slowly rolled to the back of her head. I dragged the knife back through, creating a clean cut, and slowly pulled the knife out. I turned around and looked Tommy in his eyes. It looked to me like he was enjoying this. His dick print was loud and clear.

Grabbing a hold of the triangle piece, I

carved out that bitch's stomach. Having a piece of her in the palm of my hand gave me a feeling that shook the marrow in my bones.

I asked Tommy to meet me at the house. I needed time to handle a few things. Sitting in my car, twirling her flesh between my fingers, I was kind of turned on. Looking around the parking lot to checking my surroundings twice, it was clear no one was in sight.

I opened my mouth and slithered my tongue from the bottom of my mouth, licking her bellybutton and wrapping my tongue around the triangle piece of her flesh. I squeezed it until the blood was flowing into my mouth, tasting better than the food we eat in restaurants.

A loud scream came from behind.

"Help! Help me!"

Dropping the flesh in my hand and pulling my tongue back in my mouth, I took a quick look around.

It was a white girl running through the

parking lot, looking like she was pulling her hair out because of a horrible wedding. The white girl began knocking on my window. I unlocked the car door just to be nice. She jumped in screaming, crying, with snot falling from her nose. I quickly handed her a napkin. I could not look at that shit.

We exited the parking lot; I needed her to feel safe so she could tell me what the fuck was going on. Looking at her in my review mirror, I asked her "What is going on?"

She replied in a panic "It is this guy."

She could barely speak. I told her to calm down.

She continued, "He is running around town kidnapping pretty females, locking them in a basement, getting us pregnant, and forcing us to have his kids. If the kid is not what he wants, he cuts the babies into tiny pieces then feeds them to us."

Tears still flowing from her eyes, what she was telling me was fucked up. But I did not get the part when she said he made them eat the babies.

I asked her "Why don't you not eat the babies?"

"He starves us for weeks; we have no choice if we want to survive."

This was a fucked-up situation.

I asked her "Who is doing this?"

"Some guy," she replied.

I kept the questions coming.

"How many girls?"

"Sixty six."

My foot accidentally stomped on the brakes. The car swerved. I had no choice but to pull over. Turning around and looking at this girl fully, I could see she was at least five months pregnant.

I sighed, looking into her eyes. She was afraid.

I said "Okay, can you take me to this place?"

"I don't want to go back there."

I looked at her rubbing her arms like it was

zero degrees in the car. I reminded her of the situation she had just escaped from. I said to the white girl "Those girls need to escape like you have. Help me help them as I have helped you."

She replied, "Okay."

The white girl started directing me. The first thing I had to do was put the car in reverse and turn round.

After almost an hour on the road I looked in the review mirror and asked her "Are you sure you remember?"

The white girl was looking nervous. Pointing at a mansion, she replied "It's right there."

I could not wrap my head around this situation.

"Do you know what this guy looks like?"

"We never get to see him; he leaves directions on a recording."

I told her to stay behind me so that I could protect her. Approaching the door, I knocked and waited patiently. There was no answer.

I continued to check out the premises. Walking around to the back, I saw there were ten-foot wire fences covered in razor points. There was a master lock on a door that led to a basement or a closet. The white girl pointed at the door with the lock.

"That is where whoever is doing this is holding the female slaves," she whispered.

If no one wants to answer, so be it. I will go in myself.

Going back to the car, the white girl followed me a little too close. But I understood she was scared. I explained to her "I will break in the house."

She instantly starts shaking her head no.

I continued, "I have to go inside and try to free these girls. You can stay in the car but what if someone comes while I am inside? They will take you."

The girl wiped her face and said "Okay, let's do it."

Using some tools, I broke inside the house. The entire house was spotless - no furniture, no soul, and no flavor. I checked behind me to make sure the white girl hadn't got snatched up. She pointed out the basement. The door squeaked as the door slowly opened up. We both went down together, one step at a time. Seeing this with my own eyes was unbelievable. There were a dozen babies and over a dozen girls tied up, legs open, and pregnant.

When I was seen by the girls, they all started screaming for help. I continued to try to make this make sense to me. Making my way to the desk, there was a recorder, papers, duct tape, and a pair of scissors. Blood dripped from all the objects.

I flipped through some of the papers.

Wait a minute. This cannot be.

Pushing my hair behind my ears and moving closer to the papers, I could not believe what I was seeing - Tommy's signature.

Looking at the girl from the corner of my

eye, I did not know what to say to her.

"Are you going to help us?" she asked.

I snatched the scissors off the desk. I stuck her in the neck, pushing the sharp object until it would not go any deeper. I had to catch her from falling. Her head fell on my shoulders, blood running down my clothes. I tossed her body to the floor, tying her up against the desk. I left faster than when I came in. I didn't know what Tommy had going on but it seemed to me this had been a working project.

Finally making it home after a long day was a relief but something told me there was going to be more shit to deal with. Before I could close the front door, I could see Tommy was stretched out on the sofa.

This bitch gets to sleep while I deal with everything. What a waste of life.

Slowly walking over to Tommy, I stood over his head. Cutting his throat played in my head a few times. Unfortunately that death would be too easy for him. I wanted him to feel pain. I wanted the pits of hell to hear him scream.

I told myself "Thank you, Tommy, for giving me more time to put my blueprint together. I am going to steal every bit of the one hundred million dollars and send your ass with your father, in hell."

My eyes gazing down his body, I saw he had a bulge. Kind of hot. Spreading my legs, I pulled up my dress while I rubbed the tip of my clit. My body needed more and I had an idea.

Looking at his hard dick made me want it. I could snatch it from his pants right now, but he made me sick. I could never sleep with him again. His dick made my pussy wet. I needed some pussy to rub against. I took out the carved-out body piece I'd carved out from that bitch earlier. Looking down at the prize I held in the palm of my hands gave me a sexual feeling. I went into the bathroom and placed the piece of flesh on the counter.

I slowly took off my clothes. Naked, I

stepped into the shower. Sharing the shower with a piece of a person as I was, I guess I was not alone. Closing my eyes, I remembered how good she'd felt. Pressing the flesh against my clit, I slowly rubbed my pussy. My legs went over the tub with my pussy wide open. It still felt a little warm. I rubbed the carved-out flesh in different directions at a fast pace. I was close to squirting. My toes curled, my eyes rolled to the back of my head, my body tightened up and there it was.

"Ahhh!"

My pussy juice painted everything in the way.

Of course, his ass would still be asleep. Standing over Tommy, looking at him made me sick. I swung and started beating him in the face with the carved-out piece of flesh I'd squirted all over. Blood splattered everywhere. Tommy blocked his face, jumping off the couch.

"What is that for!?" he screamed at the top of his lungs, standing there with his chest out.

"You left me there. You left me to deal with that situation alone."

His best reply was "I thought you had it! I kept trying to get your attention but you blacked out."

I replied "So you ran off?"

I shook my head in disappointment. I warned Tommy that if he slept with a nasty bitch again without telling me, I would take all his money and kill him slowly. With that being said, I had nothing more to say. The only thing left to do was to end all of this.

Tommy brushed past me, bumping against my shoulder, then walked right into the bathroom and slammed the door. As soon as I heard the shower come on, I knew this was the perfect time to follow the blueprint I had been preparing, planning, and rehearsing for years. I was over the games, over the unhappiness, the bad sex, and the worthless conversations. I, Kacy, was feeling different, powerful and strong.

He better be lucky he gets to live one more day.

I was too busy trying to buy me a mansion. I had an appointment set for a house showing in just a few hours. I'd done what Tommy asked of me and had called a realtor earlier last week.

Leaving the house at this very second was out of my control. I was determined to buy this mansion. This realtor was to die for - dead gorgeous. The guy that had shown me the house was an ex-athlete, and Gogo boy. Watching his excitement to be able to show me this house made my pussy moist. I loved a determined man.

I am about to slow this house down a bit. I asked the sexy man "Are you married?"

He replied, "Well, uh, if you want me to be."

I smiled. He had no idea I checked him out the moment I laid eyes on him. I pointed out to him his wedding ring left a mark. Of course he laughed.

In the end I purchased it - eight bathrooms,

nine bedrooms, two living rooms and dining areas, and equipped with a chief kitchen.

Waiting patiently, I finally received the notice of a wire transfer - fifteen million dollars. Later that evening, I purchased a five-million-dollar condo, just for me and with only my name on the deed. The same night the realtor allowed me to stay the night in the condo. My body, my pussy, and my ass were very lonely. I decided to have a tiny bit of fun. I called the realtor that sold me the mansion and asked "You want some black, juicy, tight pussy?"

Chapter Thirteen: Satan is God

There was a need, a hunger to take something valuable from Tommy. His life, his inheritance, his soul. Sticking to the plan was the only thing left to do. I had to revisit the place that created me, that forced me to be something beyond human. Pulling down into the old white church where it all began, chills zip-lined down my spine. The hair on my body stood up, but the other half of me was saying *Go home, run as fast you can and never look back.*

But I knew what had to be done if I planned on living the rest of this life fruitful. I'd started this mess. If it hadn't been for me wandering off on the day of the funeral…

Taking my first step back inside the church, a breeze came across my face. The energy was different - not as heavy, not as stale. The spirits knew who I was. Something evil had adapted inside the vessel of my body. My inner self told me I was home.

Slowly backing out of the church, I ran to the trunk of my car. I opened it and looked inside. I paused for a second, thinking about just going home and enjoying my new house. But I hadn't come all this way to run. Pulling with all my strength, I dragged out the heavy gas can that I had filled with gasoline the night before. I wobbled inside, dropping the gas can onto the floor.

I took one last look around; I could feel the voices in the air mourning all the dead souls this place had collected. Placing the gasoline in the middle of the floor. I could feel the souls running loose. With my shoe I kicked the gas can over. The gas began pouring and spreading wide. I picked up the can and spread the rest of the gas through the entire church.

One more place to go…

Stepping outside, I opened the dungeon. Looking inside, I told myself "Too bad."

I dropped the gas can inside. When I heard it hit the bottom I struck a match and dropped it inside. With a grin on my face, I struck another match and tossed it inside the church. Sitting in front of the flames and watching the flames hit and pop, I screamed "Let hell return back home!"

A snarling voice came from behind me. It screamed in many voices.

"Not too fast."

The second I tried to turn around, the demon snatched me by my hair and pulled me straight up in the air. The demon pulled me closer. Looking at him face to face, in a voice of many voices it said "You will die with us."

My jaw bones began to stretch, bopping and snapping. My mouth fell open and my eyes rolled to the back of my skull. A voice had came from my soul. It said in a powerful, God-like voice "My name is Asmodeus"

This creature was ten feet tall. It tossed me across the field. My back hit into a tree, breaking my bones. The creature minimized its height to human form. Slowly walking up to me, the creature looked over at me and said "My dear child."

Looking over, the church was in flames.

The creature said to me "Not much time."

Naked, its dick was between its legs, swinging back and forth and alternately touching the left and right thigh. Screaming did nothing, and crying was pointless. I wanted to get away.

A voice in my head told me not to move. My body couldn't even twitch. The demon - now in human form and human size - pulled me to him.

"My child," the demon growled.

The creature spoke in many voices. It said to me "I need you to have a child and you will call it Cambion."

The demon forced himself on top of me, putting his hard twelve-inch dick inside of me. I could feel his oversized veins sliding past my clit. Every stroke was painful at first but then I adjusted to it. My hands slowly went on his back. My nails penetrated his skin. I began to moan.

His cum filled my stomach. My skin

stretched as if I was six months pregnant. The demon laid me down gently. He got on his knees to hold my legs open. I screamed in pain. Going inside of me with his head, he started crawling inside of me, going through my pussy. The creature wiggled its way in, breaking bones. I screamed until my voice could not scream anymore. The lower half of its body formed into a snake and it slithered the rest of its body inside of me.

I thought I was choking. I grabbed onto my throat and I felt his head turn inside of me, my eyes rolling to the back of my head. My bones began to pull themselves back into place. I didn't have any idea what was happening. Taking a swift look around, I did not recognize the area. Wherever I was, I had to get out of there, like right now. Attempting to stand on my two feet, I collapsed in my struggle. I tried to stand but my body had no strength. I did what was best for me at that moment.

Blood running down my legs, I began pulling myself into the car. Looking into the car, I saw a sticky note attached to the steering wheel. A reminder. The only place I could go and heal was my condo.

The feeling in my legs was coming back. Walking again became easy. I tried not to be seen by the front desk, but that was nearly impossible. The white lady behind the desk asked me if I was okay. I looked at her, sticking my tongue out and hissing. The lady jumped back, afraid.

Slamming my door closed, my ears began to ring. Voices filled the air.

"Get it together. Stick to the plan," voices whispered in my head.

Stumbling into the shower, I turned on the cold water. I fell inside the shower and tried to cling onto consciousness. I told myself out loud "Kacy, pull it together."

I looked down.

"Shit, Kacy."

I still had my clothes on.

I got naked and wrapped myself in a towel. I let my titties hang free. I felt more awake and better.

Noticing my multimillion-dollar condo was empty, I picked up my tablet from the countertop and I began to splurge. By the time I checked out my bill, it was a measly sixty thousand dollars. My wish list was filled with new paint, abstract female colors, pictures, and sculptures. That wasn't even counting my new car.

After a proper warm shower, I clothed myself with an all-white T-shirt long enough just to cover my waist line. Under that, I slipped on a pair of see-through panties - hot pink. I turned on my TV and while the commercials played I grabbed a wine glass that the realtor had left for me as a gift and poured a nice glass of wine. I danced around the condo celebrating endless times, and my new condo. Tommy was nowhere to be found in my brain. It was just me, myself, and this bad bitch.

While I was having my fun, there was a small knock at the door. It made me accidently spill some of my wine on my marble floor. Doing the cha cha, I slid all the way to the front door. I checked the peephole. It was two guys who looked like they were in uniform.

I cracked the door open.

"May I help you?"

One of the guys replied, "Yes, you can. We are here to deliver your furniture."

"That was fast."

I closed the door for a small moment to unlatch the rest of the locks.

One of the boys said, "Here, Miss, could you sign this for us so we can bring your stuff up?"

After I signed, the cute boy said "We will be back with your furniture."

I poked my head out the door and watched the boys fade away down the hall. I slammed the door and ran inside, burning a few candles to set the mood. I grabbed a bag of black sand from my purse and as quickly as possible I drew a pentagram in my living room.

There was a knock at the door. It was the moving guys. I yelled out, "Here I come! Give me a minute!"

I changed into a red thong and a red see-through bra. Opening up my front door, the young movers' eyes were attracted to my body. That was exactly where I needed them to be, not focused. I left the door open and took a few steps back.

"Come inside and bring everything with you."

I had to snap my fingers for them to move.

I leaned against my island, watching the boys struggle. They made small sounds while using their strength to get the furniture inside the condo.

I asked, "Where is the rest?"

The boys replied, "The rest of your furniture will come tomorrow."

As I slowly walk past the boys, I stretch my arm out and graze both of their dicks. Looking outside the door and making sure no one was there, I closed it shut.

In a sexy voice I said, "Follow me."

I pulled the boys by their belts. I could hear their feet drag along. I slowly placed myself inside the pentagram.

"Come, undress yourselves," I said to the boys.

With all three of us positioned inside the pentagram, I pointed at the cutest boy and said "I want you to suck his dick." Pointing at the other boy I told him, "I want you to suck my pussy lips."

Watching the facial expressions on the boy's face that was getting his dick sucked was turning the heat up on the little movie we were making. I moaned as the boy ate my pussy, latching my hands on his head and dragging my nails through his scalp. Slowly pushing him back, his lips were covered in my pussy juice.

I pointed at both of the boys and told them, "I want both of you to stick your big dicks inside of me. One big dick inside my pussy and the other big dick inside my fat ass."

One of the boys moaned, "I am about to cum! My dick cannot hold it! Ahh!"

His cum was warm. I felt it deep in my ass. I guess he could not get enough. He kept stroking me as deep as his big, juicy dick could go. The other boy was still stroking away, making noises, but for him it was too late. Slowly opening my mouth, my jaw bones popped out of place. My mouth was at an acute angle.

Hissing at the boys scared them. One boy tried to pull away. My tongue slithered and licked his face. His fear was tasty. My tongue jabbed one of the boys in his eyes until his eye ball rolled on my tongue. Their screams filled me with joy.

Wrapping my tongue around his friend's head and yanking his head from his shoulders, the boy was helpless. No eyes to see, no tongue to scream. I left him right there; I would use the boy as my sex slave.

Chapter Fourteen: Human Feast

I had text Tommy before the sacrifice of the boys who delivered my furniture. That was why I'd had to make the sacrifice as quickly as possible.

Me and Tommy had agreed to go car shopping. I left the condo as quickly as possible but I was running late. I jumped into the car, burning rubber to reverse, and down the road I went. I pushed seventy-six miles an hour as I swerved through cars, ran red lights and tried to make sure I met Tommy at the car lot before they closed.

Meeting Tommy at the car lot was a waste of time. We decided to keep looking until we could leave our old car behind, jumping car lot to car lot. Tommy found the Porsche he was looking for and left his old car behind. I, on the other hand, was not having any luck until the last hour at the last car lot. There she was - the perfect black on black McLaren. The windows were already limo tint. Tommy was looking at me from his car window and smiling. He probably felt good about today. The only thing that was going through my head was "You are going to die."

My pussy was horny. After spending so much money today, I needed to celebrate. Tommy pulled up beside me in our brand new, cash paid for car sitting side by side. Stretching my head out the window I yelled, "I'll see you at the mansion. I have to go make a cash deposit."

The light turned green and we cruised through the city until it was time for us to depart ways.

I was still horny and I wanted something different other than a hard, throbbing, juicy dick. I cruised though the town looking for a hoe - a bitch no one would miss.

I could not find anything I liked. I guessed I'd go to the condo, cut the boy's dick off and make use of him as much as I can. Pushing my hair behind my ear, I slowed down as the light turned red. Sitting there waiting for the green light, I looked over and there was my candy for my sweet tooth. A white snowflake, a beautiful young Tinder girl. Her ass looked nice and juicy. Her booty was hanging out her shorts, titties bouncing, nipples showing through her thin shirt. Watching her closely as she crossed the street, I wanted that pussy. I placed my hands between my legs and slowly rubbed my clit.

I screamed out the window and the girl turned around. I waved her down.

"Would you like a ride?"

I thought *Who wouldn't? I am driving a McLaren.*

The snow flake twirled and smiled. Twisting her hair she replied, "Hmm, I don't know."

I replied "It'll be fun."

She told me what I wanted to hear.

"Hmm, okay, let's go!"

I watched her closely. I could smell her flaws.

When she got into the car, I started making

conversation with her, making her believe I wanted to get to know her. All I was doing was keeping her mind off where we were going.

I slowed the car down, turning down an alley. I looked at her and said, "Don't worry, people don't come over here, unless they drive cars like this one."

She smiled, her little cheeks turning red.

I pointed down between my legs.

She asked, "What do I need to do?"

"Eat my pussy."

"For how much?"

"Ten thousand dollars."

I grabbed the white girl by her hair, pulling her head down between my legs. Her tongue was soft but strong. I ground my pussy on her lips. I pulled her head up just to look into her pretty innocent eyes. I aggressively tore open the girl's shirt and her titties fell out of her bra. I placed my face in between her juicy, fluffy titties and licked her down her chest.

The girl stuck her finger inside my pussy, stroking it in and out. I leaned my head back and moaned to the sky. I pushed her head between my legs.

"Lick my clit."

Her mouth was a golden buzzer. The girl had my legs shaking but I did not want to squirt just yet. I pushed her back, my head dropping between her legs.

I said to her, "Oh my God, you're so fucking wet!"

Taking my teeth and nibbling on the white girl's pink clit, I felt her super wet pussy. My nibbling turned into biting. She gasped and moaned. She began crying out, "Keep going, I am so close!"

I squeezed my teeth, harder and harder; I could feel the blood on the tip of my tongue.

"It hurts! Ouch!" she screamed.

I pulled on her clit as hard as I could, pulling a chunk of flesh from her pussy. Blood sprayed everywhere. Now *this* was the sex I'd been waiting for. Spreading her legs, I jumped in between them, on top of her pussy. I started scissoring on her pussy, sliding back and forth, going faster, the blood making it easier to slide on this pussy. She was really wet now. I was so close to squirting; I could not help it. I let out a loud moan, my body shaking on top of hers, my pussy releasing the rest of the cum.

Chapter Fifteen: Slaying My Husband

Kacy sent me a message earlier letting me know that some movers would be coming by the new house to drop off our furniture. I took a self-tour of the house, since I wasn't invited to the house hunt. The new house is perfect, but outside of it, we still have a lot going on. Honestly, since accepting the inheritance, I'm not sure how much longer we'll be alive. Satan is coming back to take what is his, unless I sacrifice Kacy, but that's not something I'm willing to do.

I used my phone to message Kacy, asking her how much longer until the movers arrive. Hours passed and there was still no sign of them. I had to get back to my secret house, which Kacy can't find out about. I have some girls there who are due to have my babies, and I need to be there to assist with the delivery.

I was pacing back and forth through the house, paying close attention to my watch and thinking, "Where are they?"

Kacy still hadn't replied, but suddenly there were three little knocks on the door. I ran to the front door and looked through the peephole.

Right on time, I thought to myself.

I greeted the movers, saying, "Good afternoon." They greeted me back and I continued, "Can you guys please make this as quick as possible? I could help if you want."

One of the guys replied, "No way, we've got this. Just sit back and we'll be done in a jiffy."

I stepped back and relaxed, watching the guys use their muscles as they worked. The more I watched, the more attractive they became. The first guy was extremely dark-skinned, with wavy hair, dark brown eyes, athletic, slim, tall, and a round, fat booty. The second guy, his coworker, was as white as snow, with long, curly hair, cheeks red as apples, blue eyes, a little thicker, and no booty.

Both of the boys were wearing skinny jeans so I had no way to tell who had the bigger dick. My mind was already made up who I was fucking, and who was putting their big dick inside my guts.

I said to them "Take a break, you guys. I have some water for you."

We talked for a little bit, sharing a few laughs. I put my hand in my pocket and pulled out a handful of cash. I asked both of the boys, "Do you want this?" One of them said, "Hell yea!" The other guy said, "Sure, we'll take it." I replied, "I don't know about taking it, but you could earn it."

They both looked at each other, then both asked at the same time, "How?" I smiled and began taking off my shirt, tossing it across the room. One of the boys' eyes followed my shirt, while the other kept his eyes on me. I walked up to the dark-skinned boy and he raised his arms. I pulled his shirt over his head and tossed it across the room. I reached for the other boy's arm, pulling him closer to me and sticking his hand down my pants. Pulling the white boy's head to me and landing my lips on top of his, I stuck my tongue into his mouth. The black boy joined us and all three of us French kissed each other. Together, we began taking off our clothes and leaned in to kiss each other's nipples. The white boy got on his knees and crawled towards my dick, looking at it like lunch meat. He pulled my hard, throbbing dick towards him, licking my balls and rolling them inside his mouth. The black boy crawled under me and said, "Sit on my face, I want this fat ass in my mouth." He smacked my ass cheeks and I reached over with both hands, jacking both of the boys off. They both had big, rock-hard dicks that were almost the same size, just a few inches different. I leaned over, filling my cheeks with two dicks.

I pulled my dick out from the deep inside of the white boy's mouth, bent him over, and pressed down on his lower back with the palm of my hand, forcing him to arch his ass in the air. I rubbed my face behind him, in between two fat, soft ass cheeks, stretching my tongue out until it touched his beautiful booty hole. His body shook and his moans sounded like music to my ears. His breathing grew heavy.

The black boy crawled behind me and I could feel his lips kissing each of my ass cheeks. He spit on my asshole and tried to force his throbbing, hard dick inside me. It wasn't big enough for me to moan, but it was just enough for me to feel.

Me and the boys started to turn and twist on top of each other like a pile of mating snakes. I ended up behind the black boy's fat, round booty, holding both of his cheeks in my hands, squeezing the fattest booty I'd held in a very long time. I pressed my hard, wet dick against both of his cheeks, sliding up and down, edging on this chocolate toy. I closed my eyes, imagining my dick pulsing and pumping cum deep in his guts.

My ears were ringing uncontrollably, bells playing deep inside my ear. In my peripheral vision, I could see the white boy's body collapse to the floor. I felt the wetness of blood smack my face. The black boy, whom I had bent over, took off running and leaned on the wall, screaming. Kacy slowly walked past me, not even looking in my direction.

Kacy was covered from head to toe in an all-red jumpsuit. Her arm was outstretched, holding a gun that was heavier than her arm. Her laser eye was focused on her target. I knew that the black boy was going to die. He was still in a crouched position, screaming, "Don't kill me, I don't want to die!"

Kacy began pistol-whipping him over the head repeatedly until his body became motionless, then she shot him in both of his legs.

Kacy walked up to me, staring me in the eyes. The color of her eyes faded away and her mouth slowly opened. Her jaw bones popped loudly, causing a crack from the ceiling to the floor and shifting the mansion. A tongue of a snake rose from the bottom of her mouth, slithering from her mouth.

I told Kacy, ``I should kill you," and then I

heard two loud bangs. Bang, bang. She shot me in both of my feet and I fell to the floor, bumping my head.

Kacy said, "Not before I kill you."

I started screaming and calling her out by her name. She tried to walk away, but I latched onto her ankles. She kicked her leg away and I screamed, "Where are you going?"

She replied, "The only question you should be asking right now is, where are you going?"

Kacy grabbed a gas can from outside the front door and began splashing me in the face with gasoline. She fetched a box of matches from her pocket and slowly put on a smile.

She placed the matches in my face, shaking the box back and forth. Her last words to me were, "Burn, baby, burn."

She struck a match and threw it on top of me.

The roars that arose from the burning body were

music to my ears. I stood there watching Tommy scream for his life and roll around. As soon as my foot hit the grass, I walked away and felt the wind blowing through my hair. I took a look around before entering my car. It's a shame I didn't get to enjoy this mansion and watch the house go up in flames.

I got into my car and pressed the gas pedal to the floor, speeding down the soft paved road. Looking down at my dashboard, my car was already up to ninety miles an hour. I pushed it all the way to the condo, passing a few cops. Checking my rearview mirror, no cops were pulling me over. Either they were asleep or not paying attention, eating donuts with coffee.

Taking one step inside the door, standing inside my condo gave me a feeling of safety. I took a breath in and inhaled the fresh, rich air. In the distance inside my condo, I saw a boy sitting with no eyes on his face. Looking at his posture, he had made himself comfortable. A white rag was tied around his face, keeping the blood from dripping or, for comfort, keeping the floating dust from entering the open wound.

I took a moment to look around and just noticed that this condo was not set up the way I had dreamt it would be. Right now, my options are limited to get help setting up this furniture.

Fuck, why hadn't I thought about this before I killed everyone? Well, besides the blind boy. Not going to lie, he was worthless. Not *completely* worthless. I mean, he was a guy, he did have a ball sack, and he did have a dick… so not that bad of a blind guy. Plus the whole blind thing was my fault.

Chapter Sixteen: In the Beginning

All I could remember was falling deep into the bed, the linen hugging my body, and feeling the soft warmth. Moving that furniture all by myself with no help forced me to use an extreme amount of power. My eyelids were weighing heavy and I fought to keep them open. Not right now. I was afraid of falling asleep and I lost sight of the blind boy, but that wasn't the reason I forced myself to stay awake. The boy whispered something in my ear and what he said was the reason I fought to stay awake.

The birds started falling from above, the insects exploded, the trees screamed, the ground below my toes crumbled, and the air around me twisted and folded. My eyes battered, the sun shone into my eyes, and different colored faces surrounded me. There was small chattering going on beside me. The people's uniforms were white and the girl sitting at the edge of my bed was holding a notepad.

Bells were ringing as if it were an alarm and a strong white man with strong jaw bones, a strong neck, and big hands stretched over me. As I turned my head left and right, I almost forgot where I was. The strong jawline man stopped the bell noise and said to me, "Kacy, awesome session today. I think we accomplished something here that we couldn't before." The lady sitting at the end of the couch hadn't stopped writing. Then it dawned on me that I was still in this mental health facility.

The nurse sitting down by my feet gently placed her hand on my leg and rubbed me gently. She asked, "What happened to the note that was handed to your husband by the old friend he had the affair with? Or did you ever get the chance to read it?" I pushed myself upward, going from laying my head on a pillow to sitting on my tailbone. I looked over at the nurse and then over to the doctor, the therapist, and everyone else in the room.

Behind the nurse, the therapist said, "What about the girls in the basement that your husband was breeding and forcing to have a perfect baby?"

I replied, "Can I get a cup of water?"

There was a small pause as nurses, doctors, therapists, and psychiatrists looked around the room at one another. Then the silence erupted and the therapist replied, "We will resume next week. That is enough for one week."

www.ingramcontent.com/pod-product-compliance
Lightning Source LLC
Chambersburg PA
CBHW071412150726

48000CB00001B/287